THE NECROMANCER'S LIGHT

ALSO BY TAVIA LARK

Radiance
The Necromancer's Light
The Paladin's Shadow
The Sword-Witch's Heart

Perilous Courts
Prince and Assassin
Prince in Disguise
Prince and Pawn
Prince and Bodyguard
Prince and Betrothed
Prince of Agony

Fortune Favors the Fae
Bound to the Wild Fae

RADIANCE I

Content Notes: This book contains corpses, walking corpses, and self-injury for the purpose of blood magic rituals.

To M., who wasn't sure she liked necromancers but trusted me anyway. I told you so.

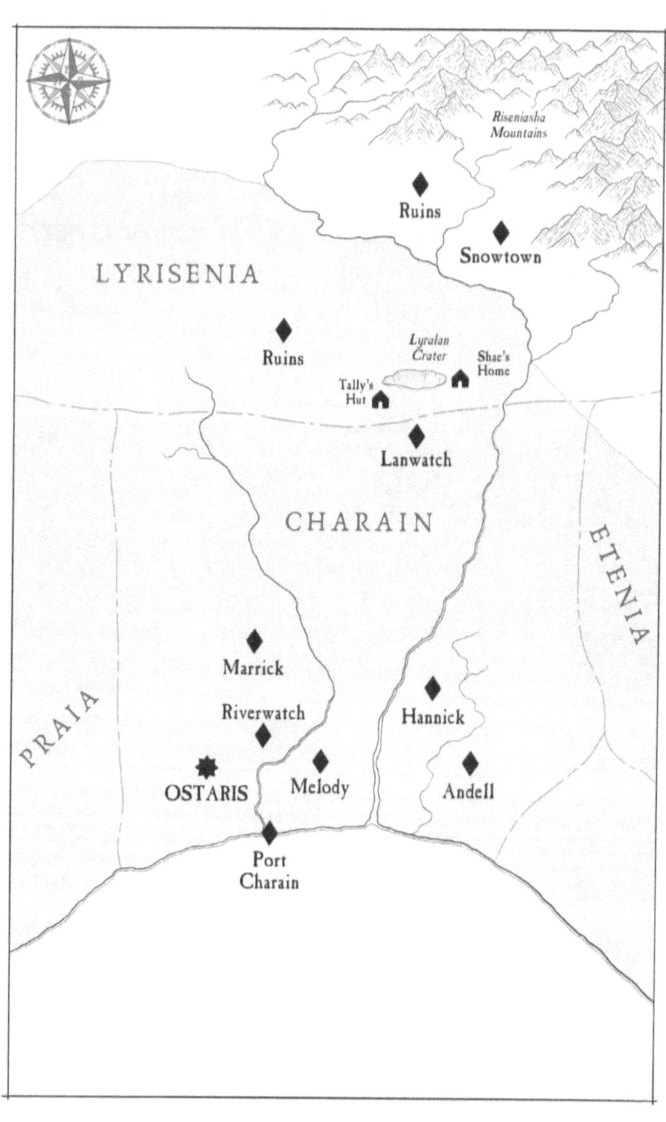

Riseniasha Mountains
Ruins
Snowtown
LYRISENIA
Ruins
Lyralan Crater
Shae's Home
Tally's Hut
Lanwatch
CHARAIN
ETENIA
Marrick
Hannick
Riverwatch
PRAIA
OSTARIS
Melody
Andell
Port Charain

SHAE

In the dying heat of the summer day, a lone figure in gray stands out from the crowd. Everyone else in the streets of Andell wears light cotton, sleeves rolled up to their elbows and collars unbuttoned. Sweat drips down tanned and freckled faces as ordinary men and women finish their day's shopping or pack up their wares. They give the dark-haired, gray-eyed wanderer a wide berth, and they try not to meet his gaze.

Shaesarenna Nightven isn't trying to hide the silver rings in his ears and on his fingers, or the silver-stitched leather bags hanging from his belt. Other kinds of mages use silver, but only one kind uses that much of it. The people of Andell know what he is.

Necromancer.

Shae shivers and pulls his coat tighter around his thin body. His silver jewelry is the only finery he owns.

His coat was once black, but it's faded to a ghostly gray over the years, and the hem is ragged. It's missing a button that he keeps forgetting to replace.

He's cold, despite the late summer heat. His magic drains more of his life force every time he uses it, and the only thing that helps is human contact. Yet that same magic drives everyone away. The thronging crowds only give him the slightest breath of warmth.

If he could take the telltale silver off, he would. The rings on his fingers hold spells to mask his presence and detect evil. The earrings help focus his control over his power, and they do something to protect what remains of his soul. The silver and amber pendant dangling from his left lobe holds enough human aura to keep him alive for a day, if he's alone in an emergency. The pendant is empty now, and it's slow to recharge as the crowd stays away from him.

He's never been to Andell before, but he finds the local Riverswords outpost easily enough. They always set up shop near the shipping yards or stables. Since Andell is landlocked, Shae follows the scent of horses. His nose leads him past the whitewashed wooden buildings surrounding the town square, through a neighborhood of older stone buildings with high arches and narrow windows. The round roof of a Moon Mother chapel rises on the northern skyline.

The mercenary guild's emblem hangs on a sign above the door: crossed swords on a blue shield.

Shae nervously tugs his worn fingerless gloves, then pushes inside. The door opens on a smokey interior, more lounge and dining hall than anything else. There's a desk across from the front door with nobody at it; the only current inhabitants are five rough-looking men and women playing cards around a table to the side, drinking and laughing.

When they see the silver in Shae's ears, the laughter stops. One man drops his cards on the table and brings his mug of ale to the front desk. He's not much taller than Shae, but he's three times as wide, all muscle and scars. From the unfriendly glint in his eyes as he looks Shae up and down, this isn't going to go well.

Shae takes a deep breath and steels his nerves. He knows rejection when he sees it, but he's too dumb or too stubborn not to try. Or too desperate. He can't get all the way to Lyrisenia without a companion. He'll die alone and frozen in the woods if he tries.

And he has to get to Lyrisenia.

"What brings you here today?" the mercenary says, settling into the chair behind the desk. He swigs from his mug, leaving a line of foam across his lip. "Necromancer."

Shae lifts his chin. "I need to hire a bodyguard for a month's journey. If you don't have anyone free for the full time, then just long enough to get me to the next outpost north."

A thick, leatherbound book sits on the desk. Shae's been to enough Riverswords outposts to recognize the local log of assignments. The mercenary doesn't even bother to flip through it; he sets his tankard on top of the unopened book.

"Unfortunately," he drawls, "we're all booked for the next six months. If your coin is good, we can see if we can slot you in then."

Laughter sounds from across the room. Shae can't help glancing towards the other mercenaries, who know their captain is lying as well as Shae does. Most of them look away hurriedly, reluctant to make eye contact with him. Only one gray-bearded man still leers at him, making no secret of his unprofessional interest.

Shae might be desperate, but he knows when arguing is pointless, and he wouldn't trust any of these mercenaries not to abandon him in the middle of nowhere. He turns back to the mercenary captain and replies drily, "What a shame. Thank you for your time."

He strides from the building, silver jangling in his ears and disappointment tightening his lungs. *Damn it.* He's used to the cold treatment, but in most towns, Riverswords are willing to contract out an escort for him. His coin is as good as anyone else's.

That's how he found his last escort, Pavus, a surly man who drank so much he could barely swing a sword. Pavus had lasted three nights with him before leaving Shae in the middle of the night, cold and alone and miles away from the next human settlement.

The two-day walk to Andell had nearly killed him.

Shae halts on a street corner, twisting one of his rings as he tries to think. If he finds a tavernkeep who'll deign to speak with him, he can ask about anyone else who might be looking for work and isn't too picky. Come morning he can seek out an alchemist or hedgewitch too—they tend to be less discerning about the company they keep. If he's absolutely desperate, he'll hire a prostitute or a convict. He'll find someone.

He has to.

"Hey, necromancer." A raspy voice breaks his concentration. Shae whirls around, hand at his belt, and sees the leering mercenary from the outpost. The man is tall and lanky, with a straggly beard and a long, greasy tail of hair twisted behind his head. This close, he reeks of sour ale. "You need an escort, yeah?"

"Your captain said you were all booked," Shae says coldly. He's desperate, but he doesn't need to be abandoned by another drunk in the middle of the wilderness.

The man laughs. "I wasn't offering myself." He leans in closer to Shae's ear, the reek of him overpowering. Something about his gaze makes Shae's skin crawl. "Just thought I'd give you a tip. There's a Varan paladin in town, staying at the Moon's Barrel. Heard he was looking for work."

Shae blinks. The last thing he expected from this creep was something useful. "Thanks. I'll see if he's still looking."

"Happy to help," the man slurs. His eyes rake down Shae's body again, and he grabs him none too gently by the elbow. "How about I show you how to get there?"

Bile rises in Shae's throat. He glances around, but nobody is looking at them. He doubts any passerby would care even if they noticed.

"That won't be necessary."

The man smiles, and his grip tightens. "It's no trouble for me."

Fine. We'll do this the hard way. Shae forces himself to smile, knowing the expression doesn't reach his eyes, and touches the silver feather pendant hanging from his right earlobe. He starts muttering under his breath, the Lyrisenian language taking on the cadence of an incantation.

The man swears and backs away as if burned. "Corpse fucker," he snarls, spitting at Shae's feet. "Get the fuck out of here." He stumbles away, still swearing, and disappears into an alleyway.

Shae takes a moment to still his racing heart. He's almost grateful nobody's looking at him, so they can't see him sagging in relief. The incantation was just a simple prayer for good luck—thankfully enough to scare the lecher away without resorting to anything drastic.

Drastic is a sure way to get kicked out of town.

The evening sky is pink and gold above him as he sets off to find the Moon's Barrel.

ARTHUR

"Thank you, thank you." The tavernkeep shakes one of Arthur's hands with both of hers. "Your generosity is incredible. How long are you staying? You'll have a room here at the Moon's Barrel, free of charge, as long as you need."

"Please, Marion." Arthur Davorin grins and lays his other hand on top of hers. He does his best to keep his voice warm and friendly, even though the routine platitudes feel like splinters in his throat. "I'm only doing my duty as a servant of Vara. I'm not sure how long I'll be in town, but I'll pay for my room just like any traveler."

The fervor in Marion's eyes doesn't dim any, but she doesn't press the question. "If you insist, but I won't let you pay for dinner. Go sit—my girl will be out with ale and bread in a moment."

"Well, I won't refuse that. I'll be right back after I see my horse is settling in." Still smiling, Arthur extricates himself from the grateful handshake with as much finesse as he can muster. "Light guide you."

He draws the usual amount of attention as he exits, and has to stop to convey the usual number of blessings in greeting. Andell hasn't seen a paladin of the Radiant Order in a while, apparently. The city's main church worships Mother Sephine, whose acolytes give blessings much more sparingly. Marion was certainly eager enough for a purification spell on her threshold.

"I've heard talk there's a *necromancer* in town," she had faux-whispered to him, so the entire tavern could hear the gossip. "Gods only know what unsavory business he's bringing to Andell. I won't have any corpses traipsing into my inn!"

Arthur prayed over her threshold to make her happy more than anything else. Most necromancers are no more dangerous than an uncontracted hedgewitch—though, no less dangerous either—but he understands Marion's trepidation. Like all higher magics, necromancy isn't something you're born with, it's something you choose. Joining a divine order to contract with a god's magic is one thing. Contracting with a demon is something entirely different, and there are few good reasons to learn to raise the dead.

When Arthur makes his way out to the tavern's stable, he finds Duchess in the largest stall, making friends with a stablehand. The young man has clearly forgotten the muckrake leaning against the wall in favor of stroking the chestnut warhorse's silky nose. "Sorry, gorgeous, you cleaned me out," he's murmuring when Arthur gets there. "I'll bring more carrots in the morning."

"Please, my lady's spoiled enough already," Arthur says with a laugh, walking up. "I came out to see how she was doing, but I see I have nothing to worry about."

The stablehand jumps, then grins. After an appreciative once-over of Arthur's height and breadth, he strokes Duchess's nose one more time. "I assure you, sir, she'll be well taken care of here. You're a good man for checking in on her, though." He steps back and picks up the muckrake. He's good-looking, Arthur notes. Strong shoulders and an easy smile. Freckles that stand out even as the evening deepens. The sort of friendly smile and work-callused hands Arthur wouldn't mind spending an evening with.

A year ago, maybe. Before everything. Before Ronan. But he's not in the mood for distractions now.

Arthur ruffles Duchess's forelock. "She's spent the past five years taking care of me. I'm only returning the favor."

Her previous source of carrots clearly moving on, Duchess's ears flick expectantly towards Arthur. He laughs and rummages through his belt pouch for a treat. She delicately lips it from the palm of his hand.

"Well, I'll leave you to your audience with Her Majesty," the stablehand says with a laugh. "I have another hour left of work. The name's Wyatt, by the way."

The way he smiles is an invitation, clear as daylight.

"I'm Arthur. You have a good night, Wyatt." His answer is polite, but just as clear. Wyatt's smile turns a little wistful before he leaves for the back of the barn.

When he's out of earshot, Arthur sighs and leans his forehead against Duchess's muscular neck.

He never thought playing the paladin would be so hard, when that was all he ever dreamed of. He joined the order seven years ago at age eighteen—the minute he was old enough to get in. Two years after that, he finished training and earned his pendant, and he was ready to save the world and bring glory to Radiant Vara, wherever the light called him. And he'd done that. He'd helped people. He was good at his calling.

Then he threw it all away for an easy smile and a knife in his back.

He paid the price for carelessness, not treason. Instead of a prison sentence, he has a year of exile from all Varan churches, before he returns for his final trial. He might have preferred prison instead of a year of wandering the countryside, all on his own, taking any righteous job offered to him. It's hard to bless farms and taverns and village babes when he feels farther from Vara's Radiance than he's ever been.

"Thanks, Duchess," Arthur murmurs, pulling away. "You be good for the stablehands here, all right?"

She nudges his shoulder. He laughs and produces one last treat before heading back into the tavern. The dining room isn't full yet, but working men and women are starting to come off their shifts, and the air is loud with laughter and fragrant with fresh food.

Finding an empty table by the fire, Arthur barely sits before a woman rushes out with ale and bread. She looks like a much-younger Marion, and he takes her to be the tavernkeep's daughter. "Sorry if I kept you waiting in the kitchen," he says with a grin. "Thank you."

"It's no trouble, sir, the cook's only just—"

The tavern door opens, then closes. Silence follows, spilling out like rippling water from the slight figure at the door.

Moments ago, Arthur would have said he prefers men like Wyatt the stablehand. Strong, working men who can play rough with a smile. Friendly. The man at the door is nothing like that. His chin-length dark hair makes a stark contrast with his features, pale as ice and twice as sharp. The golden light of the setting sun outside and the lanterns inside seem to break on the fragile lines of his face, fracturing into ethereal starlight. His lips are thin, and his dark eyes search the room.

More than anything, the young man looks lost.

Arthur notices the silver in his ears a half-second before their eyes meet. He flinches in instinctive revulsion as he recognizes the signs of a necromancer.

The second shock comes right on the heels of the first. Against the cold, a flame flickers inside his heart. A touch of divinity he hasn't felt since he was first called to Vara's service. That he feared he might never feel again. It's barely there, then gone again, and he doesn't know what it means. He doesn't know what Vara wants.

All he knows is it has something to do with the necromancer currently walking directly towards him.

SHAE

Shae spots the paladin almost immediately. The sun-blazoned white tunic over leather armor stands out like a beacon across the room. Shae nearly sags in relief—the Riverswords lecher told the truth about this, at least.

Then the paladin makes eye contact with him and flinches, and Shae's stomach drops. Typical. He steels his nerves and crosses the room, ignoring the whispers springing up around him. He can't help noticing the woman behind the bar crossing her arms in a warding gesture.

A waitress flees from the paladin's table at Shae's approach. The paladin doesn't move, except for a slight furrowing of his brow. "Do you need something, necromancer?"

Shae almost trips over his own feet.

The paladin's voice isn't friendly at all, but the low, warm timbre of it sends shivers down Shae's spine. The man is shockingly handsome—a painting come to life, all broad shoulders and square jaw, wind-mussed blond hair and a hint of stubble. But Shae barely notices that. He's too enraptured by the man's aura, the waves of warm and light coming from him. They're not even touching, but Shae feels warmer than he has in months.

Hoping his desperation doesn't show on his face, Shae sits down across from the paladin. "My name is Shae Nightven. I need to hire a sword, and I heard you were looking for work."

The paladin raises a perfectly rugged eyebrow. "I'm Arthur Davorin of the Radiant Order," he says after a moment. "And I heard there was a necromancer wandering around town scaring folks."

Shae folds his hands together on the table, stomach twisting with hope and worry in turn. The paladin—Arthur—certainly sounds skeptical. But he hasn't rejected Shae yet. This is the worst part, the wondering and waiting, before someone leaves.

"The sooner I hire someone, the sooner I leave." As much as he wants to make a good impression, Shae can't quite keep the exasperation from his voice. "And the sooner I can stop scaring these pitiful souls."

To his surprise, Arthur chuckles. He leans forward with one forearm on the table, searching Shae's face for something. There's a slight flicker of warmth, energy passing through Shae. Nothing harmful, or Shae's rings would have deflected it. Probably some sort of detection spell—with the unintended side effect of making Shae's heart race. He's never felt

Varan magic before. Never tasted so much sunlight from one person.

"My sword might be available, then," Arthur says eventually. Still skeptical. "If the task doesn't run counter to my oath."

Shae has definitely never hired a man like this before. Arthur hasn't even asked the price or the length of the journey. "I don't need help raising the dead and terrorizing the peasantry," Shae says tiredly, then hesitates. If he asks for too much, will Arthur turn him down? But if he asks for too little, the man won't believe him. He's heard tell that Varan paladins can sense truth and lies. In the end, he lowers his voice, so nobody else in the tavern can hear. "I'm going to Lyrisenia, where I want to banish a demon. I can handle the demon, but I need protection on the journey there."

If I can't handle Izen, I'm dead anyway.

Arthur gives him another long glance, then sips from his tankard. "All right. As long as we're not terrorizing the peasantry." He stretches his hand across the table.

Shae stares at it. The worn edges of the metal gauntlet and the well-kept gleam of the leather gloves. He hasn't even named a price yet, and the paladin wants to shake his hand.

"One gold a day, and twenty more when the task is done," Shae says, wanting everything laid out clearly. "The journey could take anywhere from three weeks to a month."

"All right," Arthur says again. "It's a deal." He keeps his hand out.

Shae half expects Arthur to yank his hand away as soon as he remembers what Shae is. But their hands meet across the table, Shae's dwarfed in Arthur's larger grasp. His bare fingertips press the leather at Arthur's wrist, and heat flows through his palm into his veins. Arthur grips his hand firmly and lets go quickly, leaving Shae dazed.

No, that isn't just the handshake leaving him dazed. His head feels suddenly light, and his stomach clenches painfully. He remembers he hasn't eaten today, or slept more than an hour at a time in the past three days. He was in too much of a rush to reach Andell before the cold took him.

Shae unbuttons his coat enough to draw a coin purse from his inner pocket. Not the one with the gold pieces; he pulls out a few coppers and flips them onto the table in front of Arthur. "Great. Now, take this and buy me dinner."

Arthur cocks his head. "You hired a bodyguard, not a servant."

Shae's lips tighten. He doesn't want to whine in front of this gorgeous fireplace of a man. He has too much pride left to explain that the tavernkeep won't serve him—he saw it clear in her eyes as he entered. "We'll need a room with two beds as well, unless you want to sleep on the road tonight."

Arthur sighs, gathers the coin, and heads for the bar. Shae keeps his head down and avails himself of a slice of Arthur's bread while he's gone. He knows he's being rude. His mother would rap his knuckles if she were alive to see him like this. But Shae's so hungry, he doesn't care. He forces himself to eat slowly, and he's only taken a few bites when Arthur sits back down heavily in front of him. The same waitress as before follows behind, setting down a tray with two bowls of stew and a plate of chicken.

"Enjoy, sir," she says to Arthur. Shae doesn't look up to see whether she spares him a glance, just reaches for a bowl and spoon.

Coins rattle on the table in front of him, making Shae jump. "Nice lady," Arthur comments. "She wouldn't take the coin."

Shae retrieves the coppers with a frown. He highly doubts the tavernkeep was nice about it. More likely she didn't want to touch a necromancer's coin.

Arthur starts digging into his own food, and they eat in silence.

$$\mathrm{)O(}$$

SHAE'S EXHAUSTED BY the time the waitress— her name is Ilora and she's the tavernkeep's daughter, Shae learns from her conversation with Arthur, who is predictably good at talking to people—leads them upstairs. She's braver than her mother if she's willing to come within arm's reach of Shae, but she still doesn't say much to him, and she leaves as soon as they reach their room.

Slumping on the edge of the nearest bed, Shae starts unlacing his boots. He hears Arthur pulling off his own boots across the room, then rustling fabric as he unpacks or repacks his belongings. A nervous tremble runs through Shae's hands, and he resists the urge to hide his boots and coin under a floorboard.

He's had to hire some shitty bodyguards over the years. The man who stole his boots in the middle of the night was probably his least favorite of them. That and other bad escorts have made Shae always nervous the first night he shares a room with a stranger. But it can't be helped. It's not like he can sleep well alone.

He sets his second boot on the floor and stretches out his sore legs.

"What time do we need to head out tomorrow?" Arthur asks.

Shae looks up and *stares*.

The paladin has taken off rather more than just his boots. He stands in the center of the room clad only in a pair of breeches, the thin fabric serving to accentuate the muscular lines of his body. In the lantern light, his rippling abs look washed with gold. Shae's eyes linger on a golden disc hanging from his neck, glinting against the coarse hair of his broad chest. He wonders if the metal is warm from the heat of Arthur's body.

"Necromancer?"

The word cuts through Shae's distraction like an ice-cold knife. Of course. This gloriously handsome man only sees Shae as a necromancer, a degenerate grave-digger. Arthur may be nice to look at, and his aura may be intoxicating, but he's no different from anyone else Shae's met since becoming what he is. Shae can't let himself get attached; it will only hurt more when Arthur leaves him.

"I'd like to be out of town by noon, but the earlier the better," Shae says, remembering the question. He forces his gaze down and away from the distracting abs, and unbuckles his coat. *The earlier we leave, the less chance you have to change your mind.* "Wake me if you're up before me. And..."

Don't leave me alone.

After a moment, there's a creak of wood and mattress as Arthur sits on the other bed. "And?"

Shae shakes his head, still avoiding Arthur's gaze. "Never mind. Goodnight." He crawls into bed, still dressed in his shirt and trousers, and curls up with his back to Arthur. Closing his eyes, he listens intently as heavy footsteps crisscross the room, pouring water and moving bags. Arthur's presence, even without words, fills the room. His warmth surrounds Shae from the tips of his fingers to the depths of his soul, and it's not as good as touching him would be, but it's enough to ease the cold from Shae's aching bones.

Exhaustion carries Shae headlong into uneasy dreams until piercing pain wakes him in the dead of night. A quick cold snap like a broken bone, except the pain slices far deeper into his soul. Shae's fists clench, and he goes rigid in bed. Breathes. Tries to breathe. Tries to count, but he can't get past one, one, one, his eyes wide open.

The shadowed room isn't as dark as the fear seizing his heart.

He knows what this pain is, and he knows it will pass. It's the reason he's returning to Charain and Lyrisenia now, after years of wandering abroad and running from remembered hurts. Another line of the binding array has broken. If the whole thing falls, Izen will be free.

And Shae will be stuck with this cursed magic forever.

The pain fades more quickly than usual. He hears another set of breaths from across the room, and it's easier to listen to them than his own. Shae closes his eyes again, and when the shivering stops, he counts Arthur's breaths until he falls asleep.

ARTHUR

By morning, Arthur thoroughly regrets agreeing to this job. He's shared rooms with clients before, but never with anyone who tossed and turned as much as Shae did. More than once, Arthur lay awake staring at the ceiling and fantasizing about tying the necromancer up from head to toe, so he couldn't keep thrashing about in his sleep.

Arthur had really expected Shae to sleep like a rock. The man looked absolutely exhausted over dinner. Dark magic must take a lot of effort.

At least Arthur's annoyance at Shae keeps him from ruminating over Ronan, the way he spends most nights.

Arthur rises with the sun, long years of training turned habit. He faces east—a plain wooden wall—and silently recites the morning prayer. The words feel like habit too. They don't have the same reverent resonance they had when he first learned them. It's foolish to hope he'll have an answer, an echo of last night's flame in his heart, but he's still disappointed to get nothing.

Once he dresses, he moves to Shae's bedside, intending to shake him awake as requested. But one look at him stops Arthur short. Finally fast asleep and not tossing and turning, Shae looks like a completely different person from the prickly necromancer Arthur met the night before. His face is softer, his lips barely parted and his long lashes kissing his cheeks. Beneath his pale skin, delicate purple shadows circle his eyes. He hasn't taken off his gloves, and his thin fingers clasp before him as if bound.

He still looks exhausted. Necromancer or no, Arthur doesn't have the heart to wake him. He'll go downstairs alone and bring breakfast back up. Shae will probably be grateful he doesn't have to talk to people, judging by the way he avoided Marion and Ilora last night.

The trip barely takes ten minutes, and five of those are spent chatting with Marion and reassuring her that he's keeping an eye on the wicked necromancer. Her fears are overblown and more superstition than anything else, but it's easier to reassure her than correct her.

Arthur returns laden with a tray of food to find Shae awake, perched on the edge of his bed. The moment Arthur opens the door, the necromancer whips his head around and leaps to his feet.

"Where the fuck were you?" Shae snaps.

There's something almost funny about the skinny necromancer trying to menace him, like a kitten with his fur bristling. Arthur sets the tray on the table. "Just grabbing breakfast. You looked like you could use some extra sleep."

The way Shae hisses at him does nothing to dispel the impression of an angry kitten. He stalks up and jabs his finger into Arthur's chest. "I told you to wake me up. I didn't hire you to disappear on me."

Arthur takes a deep breath. Kitten or no, he needs to set some boundaries.

"You hired me as a bodyguard, not a nursemaid," Arthur growls, grabbing Shae's narrow wrist. Not hard—he knows his own strength very well—but Shae freezes, wide-eyed and silent, at the touch. "You were perfectly safe in here. If you weren't, we wouldn't have stayed at this inn. Unless there's something you're not telling me, which is on you."

Shae's elfin features flush pink. Anger or embarrassment. He stays frozen a moment longer before yanking his arm away, rubbing his wrist even though Arthur knows he didn't grab it hard enough to hurt. His gaze goes distant, and he doesn't say anything.

Arthur crosses his arms. "I'm serious. If there's anything about this job I need to know, you need to tell me. Otherwise, I'm out."

"Of course," Shae says stiffly. "My apologies. I had intended to tell you more as we traveled."

"I'd prefer if you told me now." Arthur sits down at the table and starts separating out his portion of egg and sausage. He glances at Shae's cold expression again, then sighs and touches his pendant through his shirt. The breath sinks into his magic and rises with the familiar sunlight-warmth in his heart. Just a touch.

The only outward sign is a brief glimmer in the air. "I'll know if you lie to me."

From the way Shae jumps, he feels the spell. For a second, Arthur wonders if he might have accidentally hurt the necromancer—necromancy is dark magic, and Vara's Radiance is the purest of light. But Shae doesn't look pained, just surprised.

"Is this a truth spell?"

"Yes." Arthur pushes some food onto another plate for Shae. "It won't make you answer anything against your will, and it won't make you tell the truth. I'll just know if you lie."

Shae's nose wrinkles. "Fine. The demon I spoke of is bound in an array in Lyrisenia, but he can possess dead creatures for a certain radius. I fear that radius has grown wider over the past few years, and I know the array holding him is weakening." He sits down across from Arthur. "Despite all my warding, the closer I get, the harder it is to hide. I don't know if he will see me coming and send his corpses to finish me off early."

There's no change in the faint ball of sun-warmth settled around Arthur's heart. The necromancer's telling the truth, so far.

"Do you know his name?" Arthur sets down his fork. "Is he your patron?"

"His name is Izen. Don't repeat it out loud—these rings are the only reason I can say it without him hearing." Shae waves his left hand, the rings in question heavy around his thin fingers. "And… yes. We have a history. I prefer not to talk about that."

There are codes of conduct around use of the truth spell. Even without them, Arthur doesn't want to push.

He just wants to know if he's being lied to, not drag the necromancer's dark secrets out of him. "Fair enough. Is it likely you'll be ambushed by corpses in the middle of town? Do I need to be ready for battle before breakfast?"

Shae looks down. "I don't know."

The truth.

"It's all right if we separate briefly. As long as I know where you are, I'll be fine."

That's a lie. Arthur's magic ripples cold.

The only lie Shae's told, and it doesn't make sense. It's the most normal thing the necromancer's said all morning—why would it be a lie? But Arthur's gotten the information he wanted. Fighting down his curiosity, he releases the spell.

Again Shae flinches, almost imperceptibly.

"Sorry about that," Arthur says cheerfully, not feeling sorry at all. "I hope you can understand my concerns."

"It's fine," Shae mutters.

It's impossible to tell whether that's a lie as well.

)O(

"HEY, PRINCESS," ARTHUR calls out as they enter the stables. Dust swirls gold in the morning light, and Duchess's elegant nose immediately appears from the stall window. "Have you finished your breakfast yet?"

Evidently so. Instead of dropping her head behind the stall door to continue eating, her ears remain pointed expectantly in his direction. Arthur laughs and steps forward to stroke her nose.

The stablehand's voice sounds from the tack room at the end of the barn. "Are you leaving? Give me a second, I'll get her tacked up for..."

Wyatt emerges from the tack room only to stop short, voice trailing off. His handsome freckled face whitens as if seeing a ghost, and Arthur's confused for a moment before he remembers the necromancer lurking behind him. He glances over his shoulder to see Shae's face twisting in a scowl.

"That would be great," Arthur says with a smile. "We're ready to head out."

But Wyatt's no longer the cheerful, friendly man who flirted with Arthur the night before. His shock settles into a grim expression. "Sorry, I just remembered Ilora needed me in the kitchen. Your tack's all in there, you can grab it yourself."

Arthur doesn't need any magic to know he's lying, but he doesn't call him on it. "All right. Thanks for taking care of my girl."

"Of course, sir. You have a safe journey."

Unfortunately for Wyatt, the nearest route to the inn is beyond the pair of them. He has to walk right past them to get out, and just as he's passing them, Shae says, deadpan, "Boo."

Wyatt jumps half out of his skin and sprints the rest of the way to the inn.

Arthur sighs. "That wasn't necessary." He's getting the sense that Shae doesn't get along well with people. Probably safest not to ask if he'd ever considered the problem might be his personality as much as the necromancy. "Come on, let me introduce you to Duchess."

It's Shae's turn to look nervous now. He steps up to the stall, but still hangs back a bit behind Arthur. "She's… pretty."

There are a lot of other words hiding in that pause, Arthur figures. Big. Scary. Seriously big. Duchess stands seventeen hands at the shoulders, and she's all muscle. Shae's far from the first person to find her intimidating. But if Shae has an issue with his horse, this job is going to be a problem.

"I'm guessing you don't spend a lot of time around horses."

"We didn't have them growing up," Shae answers. "I don't know how to ride."

"If everything goes well you won't need to." Arthur scratches under her forelock, and she leans into the petting. She hasn't even looked at Shae yet, focused completely on Arthur. "Mostly she'll just be carrying our packs, and we'll walk unless we need a quick get-away. Here, give her this."

He holds a cookie out to Shae. Duchess's ears immediately swivel in the necromancer's direction, finally acknowledging his existence.

"Lay your hand out flat and move slow. She won't bite." Thanks to very careful training, but Shae doesn't need to know about that.

Arthur steps back and watches like a hawk as Shae edges forward. The necromancer follows Arthur's instructions to the letter, slowly offering the hard cookie in the center of his gloved palm.

Duchess delicately lips the cookie from his hand, barely even touching Shae. Crunching noises fill the barn, and she looks between Arthur and Shae, ready for the next treat even as she's still eating the first.

Great, Duchess likes him. Now as long as... Arthur peers at Shae's face, and all his thoughts disintegrate until they're no more than the dust in the air.

The necromancer's smiling. He's practically glowing, eyes shining as he stares up at Duchess. There's something fragile about the expression, and Arthur wonders when the last time he smiled was. Wonders what it would take to get him to smile again.

"She's so nice." Shae turns to Arthur. "Can I pet her?"

Arthur wonders how he'll survive the direct force of Shae's smile turned towards him. His blood pools low in his stomach. "Absolutely," he says gruffly. "Stay away from her ears, but feel free to pet her while I tack up."

He strides towards the tack room, fantasizing about snow and cold rivers in an attempt to bring his sudden arousal down. Not that Shae would notice, given how distracted he is by the most beautiful horse in the world. Arthur takes his time gathering his tack anyway.

Working with a necromancer is one thing. Lusting after one is something else entirely. Arthur has just a month and a half left in his penance, and anything that distracts him from his faith is dangerous.

The laws of Charain don't forbid necromancy entirely, and the doctrine of the Radiant Order doesn't forbid dealings with necromancers. But neither the government nor any of the country's faiths encourage the practice. There are too many necromancers who've progressed dangerously far beyond permitted tasks like questioning murder victims or laying wandering spirits to rest. When Arthur stands trial after his penance, he needs to be able to say with a clean heart, under the truth spell, that all he has done has been righteous. Dallying with darkness won't look good on his record at all.

Even if darkness is extremely attractive when he smiles. Arthur's made that mistake before.

SHAE

Shae barely notices Arthur walking away. He's too entranced by Duchess's extremely soft nose, and the way she wiggles her lips under his hand. His heart feels warm in a way that has nothing to do with magic or human presence. He's just…

Happy. Duchess is the first creature he's met in ten years who hasn't flinched at the sight of him. She doesn't know he's a necromancer, and she doesn't care.

Shae tries out scratching her forehead, the way he saw Arthur doing it, and sure enough, Duchess leans into the touch, big brown eyes blinking slowly. She really doesn't care who or what he is—as long as he comes with treats, probably. Her coat is so soft, the most beautiful orange-red. *Maybe learning to ride wouldn't be so bad?* He peers in the stall at the rest of her. *No, she's still gigantic. Petting is fine.*

It's a while before Arthur returns with a bucket of brushes. Shae isn't sure what took him so long. Tack must be complicated.

"Do you want help?" Shae asks.

Arthur hands him a wide-toothed comb and opens the stall door. "You can brush her mane out. Don't walk behind her."

Shae follows him into the stall, flushing at the nearness of his aura, and glances at Duchess's massive feet. He definitely wasn't planning to walk behind her.

Brushing Duchess's mane proves more difficult than it sounds; her hair is wiry and full of straw from rolling in the stall. Shae's barely done by the time Arthur grooms the entire rest of her, from picking her hooves to brushing her tail to currying out her coat and saddling her up. He's probably doing it wrong somehow, but Arthur doesn't correct him, and for once, it's hard to worry. It's soothing, combing out Duchess's mane while she pats him down for treats, totally uninterested in the silver on his fingers and ears.

And with Arthur so close, Shae is almost warm. When he closes his eyes, his wrist still burns sweet from the grasp earlier this morning.

Don't get too comfortable, he warns himself. Arthur's horse might be the most miraculous creature Shae's ever met, but he's still not sure about Arthur himself. The man's aura is so warm that Shae craves him with every fiber of his soul. He wants to curl up in his arms and press his forehead against his heartbeat and absorb every bit of light and heat from him.

But this morning, Shae woke up to the familiar cold spilling into his heart. He woke up alone.

I'll take what I can get, but I can't trust him.

☽○☾

AS THEY LEAVE town a few hours later, Shae's shoulders lighten in relief. He needs human contact, but the fear and revulsion are a different kind of cold he can never quite shake. Better to be on the road, walking towards his goal, with just one person by his side. Even if that person's being paid to be there.

Another month and this will be over. One way or another.

Most of the people he's paid over the last few months have been quiet travelers. Except for Pavus, who would get drunk and talk to himself in Praian, a language Shae only recognizes the curses from. At first, Shae thinks Arthur will be the same way; they don't talk for the first hour or so out of town.

Then Arthur calls for a rest beneath a huge, shady tree. "It's hot out," he says, letting Duchess munch on a stretch of grass. "You're going to pass out if we push until noon."

"Fine." Shae doesn't feel like explaining that he only knows it's hot by the sweat beading on Arthur's temple. The gleam against his tanned skin.

"What is it?" Arthur asks, and Shae realizes he's been staring.

Fuck. He covers with the first question that pops into his head. "How long have you been a paladin?"

Which seems basic enough, but Arthur winces. "Seven years. I joined the order as soon as I could, when I turned eighteen." He continues lightly, fiddling with Duchess's mane. "But I'm technically out on penance, now."

Shae stares again. He never expected to hear that tone of voice from Arthur. The tone he himself has used so often. Casual words covering up hurts he doesn't want anyone else to see.

He forces himself to look away. He can't force himself not to ask, "What does that mean?"

"It means I trusted the wrong man, and he brought harm to the order." Arthur shakes his head and laughs bitterly. "Sorry, that's so vague. He used me to get into the temple, and he stole a relic. He killed a priest while he was escaping. I was deemed involved but not responsible, so I was sentenced to a year of penance before my final trial."

"Does penance mean you have to say yes when random necromancers want to hire you?"

"I can do almost anything besides set foot in a church," Arthur says, and there's that barely hidden hurt again. Arthur clearly isn't as used to masking his feelings as Shae is.

Shae isn't sure how to feel. Killed a priest? Penance? The words seem strange under the bright sunlight, coming from Arthur's handsome face. Shae can't fathom sharing his own hurts so openly. "You didn't have to tell me that."

Arthur shrugs. "Wouldn't be much penance if I kept it a secret." He cocks his head, some of the darkness fading from his eyes. "You don't seem bothered by it, though."

It's Shae's turn to shrug. "I guess I've seen worse."

"I bet you have." Arthur takes a swig from his water flask. "Fair's fair. How long have you been a necromancer?"

Shae is distracted by the way Arthur's head tips back, stretching out the line of his neck. The way a bead of sweat gleams down his throat. He's so distracted that when he hears Arthur's question, he answers truthfully.

"Ten years."

When Arthur's brow furrows, Shae realizes his mistake. The man isn't stupid, and the math is easy. Sure enough, Arthur's next question gets to the heart of the matter.

"Wait, how old are you?"

Images flash before Shae's eyes. Dirt under his nails. Scattered bones. Blood seeping from the cracks of his skin to the cracks of the earth. His only connection to those he called. His breath frosts the air as the cold comes for him.

Shae shakes himself. The cold never leaves, but the day is bright and the road ahead is long. He tosses his apple core beneath the tree. "None of your business," he snaps. "Let's go." He strides back to the road without waiting for Arthur and Duchess to get moving.

Arthur might be thrilled to share his own dark past, but Shae feels no obligation to return the favor. His penance still hurts plenty when he keeps it secret. He doesn't need to tell the truth. He just needs to undo his mistake and forget all of this ever happened.

)O(

THEY DON'T TALK much the rest of the day, which is fine by Shae. He can tell Arthur's going a bit stir-crazy from the quiet, though, by the way his conversations with Duchess get more and more frequent as the day wears on.

They set up camp by a river, which Arthur tells Duchess is a small branch of the Rising Run. Shae recognizes the name from his map, and glances along the rippling current. The Rising Run begins in the Riseniasha Mountains and carries through the heart of Lyrisenia, then through Charain until it pours into the ocean. These very drops of water have passed through Izen's domain. They've seen Shae's destination.

"I'm going to bathe," Arthur says after getting a fire started. "I'll be right over there."

Shae nods and sits down by the fire. The river's easily visible from their campsite, only a few thin trees between him and the waterline, but he appreciates the heads-up, compared to the unexpected vanishing he woke up to this morning. He's barely explained anything—he knows he's being a tightlipped asshole about it—but Arthur's still listening and adapting to what he says.

The paladin's probably the nicest bodyguard Shae's ever hired. The worst part is that it won't matter. He'll still leave in the end. Everyone does.

Enough moping. Shae scoots a little closer to the fire, until he's nearly singeing his toes in a bid for warmth, and glances out towards the river.

He sees an expanse of gleaming golden skin, and hurriedly looks away.

Then looks again.

He's only human, after all, and Arthur's broad, bare back is glorious. Even from this distance, Shae's entranced by the way the muscles move over his shoulders, the way his broad shoulders narrow to his waist. The slight difference in skin tone at the boundary between waist and—

Shae can't remember the last time he saw another man's bare ass, but he's very sure he's never seen one as fine as Arthur's. His own body flushes with a heat that has nothing to do with the fire, and he turns his head sharply away before Arthur turns around and notices his inappropriate leering.

We're both men, we're traveling together, this is normal, right?

He sneaks one more glance just in time to see Arthur wading into the running water, and he leaps away from the fire to the opposite side of camp. Visions of wet, golden skin rush through his mind anyway. He rubs his gloved palms over his eyes, trying to chase them away. "No, no, no," he hisses to himself. "Bad Shae."

He can't imagine a righteous Varan would react kindly to a necromancer leering at him like that. Working together is one thing. Shae's inappropriate fantasies are quite another.

Not that he would know how to act on them, even if he wasn't scared of chasing Arthur away. He's had neither the will nor the opportunity to pursue any sort of friendship, much less a lover. The only people interested in him have been people like that River-swords mercenary back in Andell. The type who'll go for anyone, as long as they're too weak and alone to fight back.

A low nickering cuts through his confused arousal. Shae turns to Duchess, tethered on the edge of camp. She's completely untacked—the first thing Arthur did when they stopped for the night—save her halter, and while she's been spending the evening trimming the grass around her, now she stares at Shae with her ears pricked forward.

"Don't look at me like that," Shae says. "I have no idea what you want."

"Cookies," Arthur says from behind him. "She definitely wants cookies."

Shae jumps and forcefully prevents himself from turning around. Arthur's probably dressed again. Probably. Shae's too afraid to find out. He stays very still as he hears Arthur rummaging through a bag. Duchess's attention zeroes in on a point just over Shae's shoulder at the sound. Then the familiar warmth of the paladin's aura surrounds him, chasing the chill from his bones.

"Here," Arthur says, right in his ear. A very bare, very damp arm emerges in his field of vision.

Shae takes the offered cookie from him and says, stiff in more ways than one, "Thanks."

He feeds the cookie to Duchess, then concentrates very, very intently on stroking her nose, and not turning around until he hears Arthur putting on a shirt.

ARTHUR

As he puts together dinner, Arthur can't help staring at the necromancer. While he understands what a great companion Duchess is, and how worthwhile and fulfilling the experience of petting her is, he can tell that's not the only reason Shae is hanging out with her instead of sitting by the fire. Shae's been extremely quiet since their conversation that morning, and he's barely willing to look at Arthur. It's clear Arthur's question is bothering him.

It's bothering Arthur, too. Ten years of necromancy, when Shae doesn't look a day older than twenty or twenty-one. Even if he was twenty-five, the same age as Arthur, that would mean he contracted with a patron demon at age fifteen.

Arthur can't imagine what would drive such a young kid to dark magic like that. He has a feeling he's not going to know for a while, if ever. Shae clearly doesn't want to talk about it.

That's fine. Arthur's a paladin, not a priest. His calling is to defend the faithful, the innocent, and the random bystander with his blade and Vara's Radiance. He has neither the duty nor the talent to help with psychological troubles.

So, why can't he stop thinking about it?

"Dinner's ready," he calls eventually, and only then does Shae leave Duchess to her own leisurely meal. Shae's cheeks are faintly pink in the firelight. Maybe he's embarrassed that he's already started talking to the horse.

Which is probably the most endearing thing about him. He's a weird, prickly bastard, but he likes Arthur's horse, and that counts for more than it should.

Necromancer, Arthur reminds himself sternly. *Not endearing. Evil, evil necromancer.*

Shae remains quiet as they eat, and he continues looking down, sideways, into the woods, towards the river, everywhere but at Arthur. That gives Arthur the opportunity to continue staring at him, trying to figure out how old he is. Twenty-five is really unlikely, Arthur eventually decides, but every number lower bothers him more and more. Dark circles show easily under Shae's pale skin, and he'd probably look even younger if he got a good night's sleep. Ate a bit better, smoothed out the sharp edges and hollow planes of his face.

After dinner, Arthur washes up and then walks a wide perimeter around their camp, hand on his pendant. He murmurs a prayer spell under his breath, calling on the Radiant for awareness and protection through the night. The answer comes not from beyond but from within his body, his Vara-contracted magic settling into a circle around the camp. If anyone touches the boundary, he'll feel it.

Shae has set out their bedrolls when Arthur returns to the fireside. "What was that I felt? A warding spell?" His face is pink again, and he isn't meeting Arthur's eyes.

"Easier than trying to keep watch with just the two of us," Arthur says. "Though Duchess makes a fine sentry herself." Then he catches up to the rest of the implications. "You could feel that?"

"Yes." Shae still doesn't meet Arthur's eyes as he sits down at the end of the bedroll and starts unlacing his boots.

Arthur frowns, and an earlier concern returns to him. "Does it hurt when I cast near you?" he asks after a moment. He's not sure how to avoid that if it does.

Shae's fingers pause at his boots. "It doesn't *hurt.*" Amusement threads through his voice. "Good night," Shae says next, quickly, before Arthur can ask anything else, and crawls into his bedroll. He turns away from Arthur, so all that's visible are narrow angles beneath the bedding and a mess of dark hair.

Arthur checks on Duchess one last time before smothering the fire in earth. The summer night is warm, and they don't need to risk drawing attention. It's so warm, in fact, that after taking off his boots, Arthur lays out on top of his bedroll instead of inside it. His head falls back on the thin pillow, and he stares up at the stars through the black lace of branches.

The night is quiet. Small creatures rustle through the underbrush, and insects sing. Duchess moves around every once in a while on her tether. The necromancer breathes next to him, slow and shallow. Arthur doesn't think he's asleep yet. They're close enough that Arthur could stretch out his hand and touch him.

Arthur's starting to feel like he's never going to figure the necromancer out. He gets pissed off when Arthur grabs breakfast, but he almost laughs when Arthur asks if he's hurt. He locks up and retreats when Arthur asks questions, but he lays out their bedrolls right next to each other. The contradictions shouldn't be a surprise; necromancers are supposed to be weird. The surprising part is that Arthur *wants* to figure him out.

He lies awake for what feels like hours until Shae's breath deepens, and the line of his body sinks slightly within the bedding. Only then does Arthur follow him into sleep.

For the first time in a long time, he doesn't dream about Ronan at all.

🌙○☽

THE NEXT MORNING, Shae looks remarkably well-rested. He still barely talks to Arthur, but the shadows beneath his eyes aren't as dark, and he moves more quickly to help pack up camp. He smiles at Duchess, which is extremely dangerous for Arthur's composure.

But Arthur has never shied away from danger. If Duchess is the key to unlocking the necromancer's icy exterior, he's happy to take advantage of that. For entirely practical reasons, not just because he's greedy for more of Shae's bewitching smiles.

They've been on the road for about twenty minutes before Arthur puts his entirely altruistic plan into motion. "Do you want to learn how to ride?"

Shae's head whips around. "Right now?"

Arthur stops, and Duchess stops with him. She likes following him, and for the most part, he doesn't even have to hold her lead when they're walking on quiet roads. "Duchess can carry you and the packs together easy." Shae's such a light, slender thing. "I'm no teacher, and we don't have enough time for anything advanced. But just knowing how to sit and stay on is a good skill to have."

He thinks Shae might refuse at first. Shae certainly glances from the height of Duchess's shoulders to the hard dirt road; it's quite the distance.

Arthur adds, "If we need to make a quick getaway at any point, I'll feel better knowing it's not your first time on a horse."

"I'd rather just kill anything that comes after us," Shae mutters. "But fine. What do I do?"

Arthur unstraps his sword from the saddle and slings it over his back, then flips the reins over Duchess's neck. She nudges at him curiously, but stays still. "All you're going to do today is sit on her and get a feel for the movement. She'll be following me the whole time."

"All right."

There are no convenient tree stumps in sight. "I'll give you a leg up. If you need to mount up when I'm not around..." He judges Shae's height again, then Duchess's. "Find a rock or something and do your best. Here, grab the horn and the back of the saddle."

Shae steps towards Duchess, which means towards Arthur, so they're sharing the same space. Arthur makes sure Shae's holding the saddle, briefly covering his thin hand with his own. They're both wearing gloves, so there's no true contact, but the touch sends shivers through Arthur's veins. Shae stiffens a bit, but doesn't pull away.

This is a great, practical idea, Arthur reminds himself. He bends and cups his hands together. "Now, put your knee in my hands and on the count of three, I'll lift while you jump. Swing your other leg up and around as you go up."

"This is a terrible idea," Shae tells him, but he puts his knee in Arthur's hands anyway.

"One, two, three—"

It's not graceful, and Arthur's very thankful for Duchess's patience, but after a moment of scrambling, Shae is safely perched in the saddle. He clutches the horn with both hands, leaning too far forward, and his coat twists awkwardly around his left leg. His eyes are very wide, and Arthur can't even pretend he doesn't find it adorable.

"What now?" Shae asks.

"Now we get you balanced. Lean back a bit, here."

Arthur reaches without thinking and feels Shae's taut stomach jump when he touches it. Pretending not to notice the flinch, he pulls Shae back into a more stable position. "Your legs go further back too, bent like this." He adjusts Shae's legs against Duchess's sides. Untwisting the coat from around Shae's thigh is definitely a practical measure, not an excuse to wrap his hands around lean muscle.

It's been a long time since Arthur's let himself get this close to anyone. Nearly a year. He wonders how long it's been for Shae.

The saddle was custom-crafted for Arthur after he got Duchess. He knows without checking that the stirrup leathers won't adjust high enough for Shae's feet to reach the irons. "Try not to randomly kick," he continues. "But keep your legs firm on her sides. Hold the reins like this."

Shae lets Arthur position his hands around the reins, thumbs up, leather slipping between the correct fingers. "I pull back to stop, right?"

"Right. She'll mostly be following me, though, so don't worry about that right now."

Shae nods and moves the reins to one hand so he can gently pat Duchess's shoulder. Then he carefully repositions his hands in the exact way Arthur showed him. "Okay. I think I'm ready to move."

Arthur touches Shae's leg one last time, even though the position is as good as it's going to get, then takes hold of a rein. "Come on, girl."

Duchess needs more of a tug than usual to get going, clearly aware of the novice on her back. She nudges Arthur's shoulder before acquiescing and taking the slowest possible step forward.

Swearing, Shae loses all semblance of posture and hunches over to grab Duchess's mane.

"Stop laughing," he hisses.

Arthur's barely even chuckling, but that sends him into a full laugh. Sure enough, his plan is working. The magic of horses is definitely the way to melt the necromancer's icy heart.

They try moving forward again, and this time Shae keeps his balance better. They settle into an easy pace, and after a few minutes, Arthur's able to devote most of his attention to the road around them instead of making sure Shae's not about to slide off.

"Hey," Shae says. Arthur looks up to see him leaning back in the saddle, looking out at the trees and the sky.

"Yeah?"

Now Shae's looking at him, a hint of a smile lighting up his face. "Thank you."

Warmth chases down Arthur's spine, and he grins back.

SHAE

Over the next few days, Shae practices riding. Mostly at the walk, and a few tries at the jolting trot. Even half an hour a day leaves him impossibly sore, but he doesn't mind. He almost regrets getting used to the way Duchess moves under him, and the way he has to move with her to stay on comfortably. The less he has to focus on the mechanics of riding, the more he's able to ruminate on the true mystery plaguing him.

Why the fuck is he being so nice to me?

It has to be some sort of paladin thing. Maybe Arthur's sworn to Vara to always be polite even to disgusting dark mages. Maybe the Radiant Order only accepts helpful human-shaped herding dogs. The man *smiles* at him. Which probably doesn't mean anything. Arthur's the sort of man who smiles at everyone.

Shae's just not used to counting as everyone.

Riding at the walk is more effort than it looks, and a while into the day's journey, Shae's ready to return to his own two feet. As soothing as it is to move along with Duchess's steady gait, he's about to reluctantly ask to get down when a flash of ice burns his right hand. He flinches.

One of his rings, alerting him to danger.

"What is it?" Arthur asks, ever observant. He tugs Duchess to a halt.

Shae drops the reins to look at his hand, touching each ring to confirm—yes, the one on his middle finger. Ghosts, restless and hungry. He tries to remember the map in his head. He's been so distracted by Arthur and learning to ride and the summer breeze in the trees and *Arthur*, but he thinks there should be a village up ahead. "How near are we to Hannick?"

"Another mile or so."

That's as far as his ring can sense. Shae twists his ring and takes stock of his strength. He feels good right now, his soul replenished by the paladin's constant warmth. He can handle a few ghosts, if the villagers don't get in his way.

"Then Hannick has a ghost problem," he says. "Uh. Help me down?"

Arthur's broad hands settle firmly around his waist, and Shae's suddenly breathless. His blood pulses towards Arthur's touch, his skin warming. He manages to swing his leg over awkwardly, then lets himself down. The ground is farther away than he remembered, and with wobbly legs, he falls back against Arthur's chest.

He jerks out of Arthur's grasp before he combusts on the spot.

Arthur slides Duchess's reins back over her head, now that Shae isn't pretending to use them. "Are ghost problems something you deal with?"

"If the locals pay me." Shae's lips twitch in an unhappy grin. "And they always pay me." If they don't, he threatens to raise the dead right back up again. That generally works very well. Arthur would probably disapprove, because Arthur's a nice person.

Shae can't afford to be nice.

☽○☾

THE GHOST PROBLEM isn't in Hannick, though. At least, not the inhabited part of it. The paladin's aura drives off the worst of the cold, but Shae still feels the grief and frustration permeating the landscape, and it leads them out onto an overgrown dirt path. The only footprints Shae sees belong to animals.

Half a mile later, they find the burned-out church. Years of rain and wind have swept away the ash, but the remaining stone walls are still blackened and crumbled, the wooden roof and doors and window frames entirely missing. The building looks like a corpse itself, and Shae can't help shuddering with the chill and stepping closer to Arthur.

Maybe too close. His arm brushes Arthur's elbow, and Arthur naturally moves away.

"This looks like a Harvest Lord chapel," Arthur says. "Hannick must have rebuilt it elsewhere after the fire."

There's no question they would have rebuilt. The people of Charain are loyal to their gods. Shae doesn't feel that sort of devotion to the divine, but he understands it.

He's about to suggest they look around back for a graveyard when another alarm ring stings his right hand. His forefinger, this time, the plain silver band that alerts for—

"Demons," Arthur says, hand on his sword hilt. "Not close, but we should be careful."

Shae forgets sometimes that Arthur has magic too, that his brilliant aura is more than just the best source of life and warmth Shae has ever found. "Let's find the graveyard quickly."

The graveyard behind the church was once fenced in, but all that remains of the fence is the occasional splintered post. Stone blocks and statues as grave markers all line up in rows, surrounded by the encroaching forest. Not all the trees are intruders, though. Shae spots the fruit trees he recognizes from other graveyards dedicated to Maiza, the Harvest Lord. More fruit trees and more gravestones climb up the hillside and farther into the forest, spilling out from the original boundaries.

"The first spell I do is just to find the right body, before I call out the ghost," Shae says. He's had to practice necromancy in front of his hired guards a few times over the past year, and he learned the hard way that it goes better if he explains some of it first. "You don't have to look at anything, especially when I'm done digging, just stay close."

Arthur loops Duchess's reins over her head and ties them up away from her feet instead of tethering her. "Is this dangerous?"

"Very." Shae shrugs out of his coat and slings it over his shoulder, then starts rolling his left shirtsleeve up to his elbow. "Only if something goes wrong, but I expect something to go wrong. There shouldn't be new ghosts in a graveyard this old."

A ghost that lingers long enough turns into a fiend or curse or parasite. Something has shaken this spirit from its place of rest within the past ten years, and Shae has a nervous feeling it's more recent than that. He glances around as he draws his knife from his belt.

"There shouldn't be demons this far from Lyrisenia either," Arthur says. "We should—what the fuck are you doing?"

Arthur seizes Shae's right wrist, stopping the knife's blade an inch away from his bare left forearm. Shae jolts, nearly dropping the blade. The paladin's familiar warmth floods through him, overriding the pain of Arthur's iron grip. His eyelids flutter, and he's half a breath from moaning at the contact.

"What the fuck?" Arthur says again, and Shae slams back into his normal state of mind.

Which is currently extremely annoyed. He yanks his arm forcibly from Arthur's grasp. "I'm practicing necromancy," he snaps. "Because I'm a necromancer. Look away if you get squeamish."

"I'm not *squeamish*," Arthur snaps back. And Shae isn't great at reading people, but Arthur looks more angry than disgusted. "Excuse me for reacting the same way anyone would react to you taking a blade to yourself."

That one sentence deflates all Shae's annoyance, leaving only confusion and a weird twinge behind his ribs. He's cut himself in front of plenty of people, clients and hired mercenaries, and they all looked away in disgust or stared in sick fascination. Not one of them ever tried to stop him.

"Sorry," Shae says after a long moment. He's not sure who's more shocked by the apology, him or Arthur. "I should have explained. I need blood to find the disturbed body. It's either that or dig up every grave on this hillside."

Arthur doesn't look happy, but he steps back to give Shae space. "Fine. Do your work."

The wind rustles through the trees, and Duchess moves to another patch of grass. The sky is a perfect eggshell blue. Were it not for the graves and Shae's sense of unease, the day would be idyllic.

Shae brings the blade to his arm again and slices, quick and shallow, a few inches from the elbow. A thin line of blood wells up immediately, bright against his fair skin. It's hardly the first mark on his arm. Faint silver and pink lines pattern his skin, most of them deliberate. Nobody's ever looked closely enough, nor cared about them, and Shae suddenly feels self-conscious with Arthur here.

But Arthur doesn't say anything else.

Shae shifts his grip on the knife and murmurs a few words in Lyrisenian. Any language would work, so he uses the tongue he grew up with to say: "Let blood call to bone. Let bone call to blood."

A tendril of cold snakes from his heart through his veins, spills out from the cut. The blood pools on the surface of his skin instead of falling, and after a moment a round drop the width of his thumbnail rises up into the air. It hangs still, trembling, then flies slowly forward.

Shae follows the drop of blood, careful to step around the graves in his way. He'd rather not disturb anyone unnecessarily. They've earned their rest. He hears Arthur following behind him, but all his attention is focused on the drop of blood leading him towards the back of the graveyard.

The blood stops at a grave right on the edge of the old fence line. An overgrown heap of earth guarded by a shoulder-height statue. The statue's arms cross over its chest, and its face looks up to the sky, but its features have long been worn away by time. Man or woman, young or old, it's impossible to say. The drop of blood falls, splashing into the crumbling soil and sinking in.

Shae waits to see if the ghost will appear, disturbed by the nearby necromancy. But the graveyard remains quiet and peaceful.

"I'm going to use a spell to dig up the grave," he says. He thinks he can spare the energy with Arthur's aura pulsing around him, and they don't have a shovel.

"Do you need help with anything?" Arthur still looks tense, and Shae can't tell whether that's disgust at disturbing a grave or lingering anger from Shae cutting his arm. But when Shae shakes his head, Arthur just takes a step back and looks out into the surrounding forest. "I'll keep watch, then."

Shae stops himself from grabbing Arthur's arm and dragging him closer. Two paces away is close enough, he shouldn't be greedy. Instead, he kneels at the foot of the grave and whispers in Lyrisenian, "Please excuse me."

Not a spell, just an apology, before he places his palms on the ground. His bare fingers dig into the cold soil, and he opens himself up to the energy remnants of the corpse below. He weaves the energy into the dirt, a foot below the surface, and lifts. The surface rises up, grass roots tearing from their moorings. He tilts the whole thing, and the earth slides to the side, piling away from Shae and Arthur.

The ghost should have appeared by now, but it hasn't.

He repeats the process layer by layer. He's maybe a foot from the coffin lid when a low growl sounds throughout the graveyard. Arthur swears, and steel sings as he unsheathes his sword. His aura pulses, blinding bright. Shae flinches, blinking rapidly, and when his vision clears, he sees Arthur lunging for the old fence line.

Facing him is a six-eyed, six-legged vaidkos.

The creature is huge, as tall at the shoulders as Arthur. A twisted cross between wolf and snake, a patchwork of ragged fur and crusted scales. Its jaws hang open, fangs gleaming, and all six of its red-and-shadow eyes fix on Shae.

Memory shudders through him. Burning eyes. A shadow caress. Cold claws in his hands, blood trickling down his wrists, a promise of power. A price he didn't understand.

Arthur's voice breaks Shae out of the reverie. "Do what you need to do," Arthur says grimly, without glancing back at Shae. "I'll take care of this fellow." He sounds tense but not panicked.

Shae really wants to trust him.

He bites his lip, sinking his hands in the grave dirt again, and finishes uncovering the coffin. There's a crash, and he can't help glancing up to see the beast pouncing forward, then lunging back as Arthur meets it with his sword. The paladin moves faster than Shae would have expected for a man that large, fast enough that the vaidkos can't take him by surprise.

In the open grave, the worn wooden coffin is now uncovered. Where is the ghost? Shae can call it back into the body even if he hasn't seen it, but that doesn't change the fact that he should have seen it. He's disturbing its body. The ghost should have tried to stop him.

A snarl reverberates through the graveyard, and Arthur yells as he drives the beast back again.

Holding his coat, Shae swings his legs around and lowers himself into the grave, still careful despite the chaos surrounding him. It's a four-foot drop from surface to coffin, and even with his careful landing, the wood creaks and splinters under his feet, barely holding his weight. He can't see the fight above anymore, but he can hear it.

"You all right down there?" Arthur calls to him. He barely sounds out of breath.

"Worry about your own skin," Shae calls back, kneeling gingerly on the coffin lid, trying to distribute his weight evenly.

He wraps his coat around his right hand, mutters another apology in Lyrisenian, and punches the wood, aiming high and to the side. Wincing as the impact shocks through his arm, he has to punch down three more times before a hole breaks in the lid. He yanks the plank up and back, until he has an open window above the skeletal face.

The body belonged to a woman, judging by the long-braided hair and the jeweled necklace slipping between her sunken ribs. What's left of her skin clings dry to her bones.

"Hello," Shae says faintly. His stomach churns. He's never going to be used to this. "Sorry to bother you, I just need to get you back to… you." He bites his lip, yanks off his left glove, and presses his palm to the dead woman's forehead. He calls on his necromancy and whispers in his birth tongue, "Come home, friend. It's time to rest."

It's as much a plea as a spell. The shadow-magic in him arcs out, sinking into the body, then bursts forth again, sweeping from the grave, seeking, seeking. Not the bright white paladin sunlight—the spirit shouldn't be far—

Shae gasps, eyes wide and unseeing, as his power slams against a blood-red torch of magic. The vaidkos. He tries to yank away, skirt around, but the spell-plea-longing dives right back. He feels it then. An ice-cold heart beating weakly in the belly of the beast.

He yanks back his hand, breaking the spell, gasping for breath. The vaidkos has eaten the woman's spirit, and it will take all the power Shae can spare to drag her back out. But if the vaidkos dies too soon, he won't be able to save the ghost.

Shae gathers enough breath to yell out, "Don't kill it yet!"

There's another crash above, splintering wood, the thunder of hooves. Something sliding through dirt, and Arthur grunts before shouting back, "Are you fucking crazy?"

"Just hold it off," Shae yells. "I'll tell you when you can kill it!" It's a lot to ask. Maybe too much. It would be easier, safer, to let this soul go. But he can't give up, not yet.

Arthur's sword swings through the air. There's a thud. But he shouts back, "Fine, but hurry it up!"

All Shae can do is trust that Arthur will do his part. He unsheathes his knife again and digs the cut in his arm a little deeper, spilling more blood down his arm. He barely feels the pain. He needs the extra power. The blood feels hot trickling down his arm as he lays his hand on the skull again, until he breathes, "Come home," and reaches out.

His blood evaporates into shadow. His eyes are open, but he can't see anything except the flow of energy surrounding him. His own darkness, Arthur's sunlight, the vaidkos's blood-red fire. The faintest hint of silver. Shae reaches for it, pouring his own life force into the magic. More and more, until all that's left is the last core of his soul, the part he's sealed safe away from the necromancy, and the gold and shadow wall he's woven around it. Everything else, he turns into a shadow blade to pierce the vaidkos's soul.

There's a collision of gold and blood flames. The vaidkos has to defend itself against Vara's Radiance. Shae's power darts forward, and he seizes the remnants of the spirit. He drags it screaming from the beast's jaws.

"Now!" Shae yells. His voice sounds thin and distant, but it tears through his throat.

He doesn't know what Arthur does. All his attention is on the remnant flying towards him, guided by his power and his blood. The spirit sinks down and *through* him, shivering down his veins. Shae's vision crystallizes to see his hand glow bright silver before the ghost sinks back into her body, again at rest.

Leaving Shae caught in the veil between life and death.

He can't feel the cold anymore. He can't feel Arthur's aura. He only feels the buzz of power beneath his skin, the exhilaration of piercing the veil. He could be a god like this, feeding off the spirits of the dead, just like the vaidkos. Greater than the vaidkos. If he just dropped the last protective wall surrounding his soul. If he turned himself fully over to Izen's gift, he wouldn't feel cold anymore.

"No," Shae whispers to himself. Grabs his arm and claws at the wound, heedless of the dirt under his nails. He needs the pain to keep himself human. "*No.*"

He drags himself from the veil and releases the power.

The vaidkos. Arthur. Everything's quiet above, and Shae can't tell who's alive or dead. He's so *cold*. He scrambles to his feet, but the movement is too much. Dizziness swims through him. He falls against the dirt wall of the grave, then slides back to his knees. Collapses completely in an ice-cold faint.

ARTHUR

rthur's blade blazes light as he sinks it into the vaidkos's chest. The creature screams at him, gray-red spittle flying from its jaws, and its six red eyes bulge out before going dark. Its legs buckle, and Arthur yanks out his sword in a spray of brackish blood before the creature collapses to the earth. As soon as the body falls limp, it begins to wither away in plumes of dark smoke, until all that's left is ash settling into the dirt.

Duchess stamps nearby, ears pricked towards the vanished monster. Her tail's up like a flag, and she looks like she's ready to fight or flee—with a preference for fleeing.

Arthur can't blame her. He feels sick from just being in the vaidkos's presence, and he knows the corruptive power would be worse if he didn't have Vara's blessing protecting him. The fight was longer than it should have been. He could have killed it quicker, if not for Shae's request.

"Necromancer?" he calls out. The graveyard is too quiet. "Shae!"

Shae doesn't answer. Arthur swears and runs, sword in hand, towards the open grave. He skids to a halt at the foot of it and looks down to see the necromancer crumpled in a heap on top of a broken coffin. Arthur swears again and drops his sword, then jumps down into the grave next to Shae.

The coffin cracks under his weight, and he falls to his knees. "Hey there, Shae, are you with me?" He reaches for Shae's wrist—one of his gloves is off, for the first time Arthur's ever seen. He yanks his own glove off too and presses his fingers to Shae's wrist, searching for a pulse.

He finds one, slow and shallow, and relief floods through him. Shae's body moves with the faint effort of breath. But his skin is still ice-cold under Arthur's hand. If Arthur couldn't feel the pulse, he would think the necromancer was dead.

He brushes the hair from Shae's cold, pale face and shakes his shoulder. "You there? Hey, wake up for me, all right?"

Shae's brow furrows, and a shiver runs through him, but he shows no sign of waking.

Arthur glances from the unconscious necromancer to the decayed corpse's face, visible through the broken coffin lid. His stomach flips, but he fights back his instinctive revulsion. He doesn't know the first thing about necromancy, and he doesn't really know what the fuck Shae did here. But Shae looks so lost and cold, so helpless, that Arthur has only one course of action. He gathers Shae up into his arms—the man really needs to eat more—and hoists him up out of the grave.

It's awkward, even as light as Shae is, and Arthur thinks surely the jostling will wake Shae up. But Shae stays completely limp as Arthur pushes him onto the surface, then clambers up after him.

"I'll take care of you later," Arthur tells the corpse, brushing dirt from his hands. Then he scoops Shae up into his arms, cradling him close to his chest.

He's so cold.

It's barely noon, but Arthur doesn't want to make even the short trek to Hannick with Shae in this state. They'll have to camp here until he recovers.

Arthur carries Shae through the open door of the burned-out chapel. The man curls up in his arms, like he's trying to get closer to Arthur, and Arthur's stomach flips again with something entirely different from revulsion.

The chapel floorplan is simple—a few back rooms behind the main worship chamber. Arthur sets Shae down against a wall in what was probably once the head priest's bedroom. There are unusable remains of furniture, narrow windows, a fireplace leading to a broken chimney. More of the roof is intact here than the rest of the church.

Arthur starts to stand up, but a tug on his tunic stops him. Shae's hands unconsciously grasping the fabric. "I'll be right back," he says, gently loosening Shae's grip. Shae's bare hand feels warmer than when he first found him in the grave, and an undue amount of relief eases Arthur's heart. He feels safe enough leaving Shae while he heads back outside.

He checks on Duchess, making sure she didn't hurt herself in the confusion. Only a patch of fur scraped away where she must have run past a fencepost. He leads her into what was probably once a vegetable garden, right outside the windows from the priest's room, and removes her packs.

Then he steels his nerve and returns to the graveside. The atmosphere in the graveyard has entirely changed. There's no more uneasiness chilling his nerves, no more whispers just out of earshot. The day is warm with sunlight and birdsong, and the uncovered grave and mound of dirt beside it are the only signs that something was ever wrong.

Arthur forces himself to jump back down into the grave to retrieve his and Shae's gloves. Shae's coat. Then he climbs out and grabs his sword from where he threw it. He'd like to cover the grave again, but he'd need to repair the coffin lid first, and that would mean looking around for tools and wood. That would take too long. A nagging feeling drives him back to Shae.

The necromancer is still huddled right where Arthur left him, unconscious against the wall. A thin, crumpled figure, looking just as ruined as the room around him. Arthur lays out a bedroll for him and then kneels at his side to check on him.

A single touch to Shae's shoulder sends a burst of fear through Arthur. The necromancer's even colder than before, the chill clear through the rough cotton of his shirt, and he's trembling under Arthur's hand. Arthur lays his palm against Shae's cheek, and the unconscious man whimpers, leaning instinctively into the touch. His expression is razor-sharp and fragile, with none of the softness of sleep.

Arthur should light a fire, but he's too scared to let go of Shae for that long. Why the hell is he so cold? Was it something the ghost did to him, or was it something he did to himself? Shae's arm lies limp in his lap, the fresh cut no longer bleeding.

Arthur slides down the wall to sit on the floor and pulls Shae into his lap. The necromancer will probably stab him for this when he wakes up, but Arthur can deal with that then. For now, he just wants the man not to freeze to death on a warm summer day. Arthur's heart hurts with the way Shae curls into him, as if desperate for touch—and with the memory of the last time he held someone like this.

Ronan was nothing like Shae. Tall, strong, darkly tanned, laughed at everything, but especially at Arthur. He liked to cuddle and trace patterns on Arthur's skin. He was sweet. He talked about his dreams of a quiet life on a farm, and he asked about Arthur's work. Far too many questions about Arthur's work, in retrospect. His sweetness was poison. His dreams were a drug.

Arthur's arms tighten instinctively, and Shae mumbles something Arthur can't understand. He isn't shivering as hard, and when Arthur touches his arm, his skin is warmer. Arthur slides his palms down to cover Shae's hands and feels the fragile bones warming under his touch.

Only then do Arthur's own shoulders loosen. The tension that's carried him through battle and aftermath fades. He tips his head back against the old stone and thinks about demons, living and dead. He says, his voice sounding rough in the ruins, "Radiant Vara, am I on the right path?"

As usual, Vara doesn't answer. It bothers Arthur in a distant, habitual way. He doesn't think this is wrong, though, holding the necromancer close. He's sworn to help those in need, and Shae is so clearly in need.

Shae's nothing like Ronan. He isn't sweet. But more and more, Arthur wants to know what bitterness tastes like.

)O(

IT'S ANOTHER TWO hours before Shae wakes. He doesn't move, exactly, just stiffens in Arthur's arms. It's gradual, and Arthur's not sure how long Shae's been awake before a tense, quiet voice says, "You can let go now."

But Shae still doesn't move, all his sharp edges held in stasis. The weight of him feels warm and comfortable against Arthur's chest. Arthur doesn't move either. "I can let go, or I can stay," Arthur says. "Do you want to get up?"

Shae's head slumps lower on Arthur's chest. "I don't want to," he says, even more quietly. Like it's a secret. "But I have to. I need to check on the grave, I need to see..."

He half falls out of Arthur's lap, then drags himself to his feet. He's unsteady from sleep or exhaustion or both. Arthur jumps to his feet too, his whole body stiff from sitting in place so long, and grabs Shae's wrist before he can go any farther.

"The dead woman can wait. We need to talk first."

Shae glares daggers at him, and it's crazy how relieved Arthur is to see that glare. All the cold fragility has melted from Shae's face, and he's flushed with anger or embarrassment. He looks alive again. "Unless you fixed her coffin while I was out, I need to do that now. It's disrespectful to leave her like this."

He's right, and arguing with him will be more trouble than it's worth. Arthur sighs. "Fine. Let's look for a shovel."

Splitting up to search would make more sense, but neither of them suggests that. Shae just trails along at Arthur's heels like a ghost himself, quiet and constant, as Arthur checks for storerooms or closets. They find a singed tool shed outside the vegetable garden, and sure enough there are a few shovels. Arthur grabs the least-splintered looking one. They can't find a hammer or nails, so Arthur ends up using the shovel as an axe to break some wooden boards from the door.

He wedges the boards over the lid of the coffin to cover the hole, then climbs back out. "Do you need to say anything?"

Shae shakes his head silently and sits down at the foot of the grave, arms around his knees. He still hasn't put his coat back on, and Arthur vividly remembers how his cold, narrow body felt tucked against his.

Arthur yanks his mind away from that distraction. He touches his heart and lifts his head to say, "May Vara's Radiance light your way." Then he picks up the shovel and starts covering the coffin.

The work is hard, but the steady movement is a relief. A chance to do something practical, something physical. The sun sinks lower as he works, and he's aching and sweating by the time he's done. He sets down the shovel and drops next to Shae, who still isn't looking at him.

Arthur leans back on his hands and looks out at the peaceful, swaying woods around them, the orchard trees heavy with fruit. "Tell me what happened."

"The vaidkos had eaten the ghost. I had to pull her out before you killed it, or she would have vanished. That's why I told you to wait." Shae grimaces. "That thing was probably the reason she woke up in the first place. There shouldn't be vaidkos this far south of the border."

That bothers Arthur too, but he's still fixated on a different problem. "I meant, why did you collapse? Do you always do that?" When Shae doesn't answer immediately, Arthur grabs his chin and forces him to face him. "You scared the shit out of me, okay? You were completely frozen. I told you before, I'm not doing this job unless I know what to expect."

Shae's eyes go wide, and Arthur feels him swallowing under his fingers. His pulse quickens. "Fine." Shae jerks away. "I don't always collapse, but it's gotten worse over the years. When I use my powers, it drains me."

Arthur can still feel the smooth texture of Shae's skin, an echo of touch against his fingers. "What should I do if I find you like that again?"

Forget Shae's smile. The way he blushes, delicate pink, is going to haunt Arthur's dreams for the next fortnight. "The same thing you did this time," he says eventually. "Human contact is the only thing that helps."

Puzzle pieces click into place. The way Shae followed close to Arthur, even when he was pissed off about something. The way he panicked that morning in the Moon's Barrel when Arthur left to get breakfast without him. The single lie he told under Arthur's truth spell: *It's all right if we separate briefly. As long as I know where you are, I'll be fine.*

"It's not just when you use your magic, is it," Arthur says slowly.

"No." Shae sounds very tired. "But most of the time, just being near people is enough. You especially—I think it's a paladin thing? You have this aura."

"So, that's why you hired me." Arthur grins. "You wanted a portable fireplace."

That startles a laugh from Shae. "Yeah, something like that."

They sit together a while, as the sun sinks lower towards the horizon. Eventually, Arthur creaks to his feet. He's going to be sore tomorrow. The fight was nothing, but shoveling isn't a movement he's used to. He reaches his hand down to Shae. "Let's have dinner. I'm starving."

Shae takes his hand and lets Arthur pull him up.

SHAE

Arthur doesn't ask any more questions as they prepare and eat dinner, and Shae is tremendously grateful for that. He still feels raw and vulnerable after saying so much at the graveside.

Maybe it's stupid to try to keep his weaknesses a secret. Arthur has a point—how can Shae expect Arthur to do what's needed if he doesn't know what that is? But Shae's never hired someone as trustworthy as Arthur before. As gods-damned nice as Arthur.

You scared the shit out of me, okay?

Nobody's cared about Shae that much since his parents, and they're ten years gone.

Shae eats his travel bread in silence and watches Arthur when he's pretty sure Arthur isn't looking at him. There's something absurdly competent about the way he performs even simple tasks like stoking a fire in the fireplace or unfastening a saddlebag. Shae's drawn to the way his hands move, the nimble strength of his fingers. He remembers how he woke up with those hands around his.

He can't stop himself from wondering how those strong hands might feel on the rest of his body, too.

There's no way Arthur feels the same sort of attraction for him. Arthur's just being nice. He's just being considerate, competent, shockingly handsome even when sweat-stained and covered in grave dirt—anyway. It's probably a good thing that someone like Arthur would never be interested in someone like Shae, because Shae isn't sure he could resist if he thought he had a chance. He doesn't need the hurt that comes with trying.

They turn in early for the night. Arthur murmurs his prayer spell, his rich voice filling the broken room, and Shae feels the paladin's magic wash through him on its way to their perimeter. His eyes flutter closed at the sensation, like invisible hands tickling beneath his chin, sliding along his waist.

Getting into bed, he's startled when Arthur lays his own bedroll out right next to his. Not even an inch of space between them. Shae's overwhelmed by the nearness of him, the scent of sweat, the sheer human heat.

"Is this all right?" Arthur asks. The room's dark, only slivers of moonlight piercing the shadows. "I figured closer is better for you."

"It's fine," Shae manages. "Yes, it's better. Thanks."

He lies down face up and wonders how the hell he's going to sleep with Arthur breathing so close to him. Now that he's had a taste of warm, strong arms surrounding him, of the steady heartbeat drumming against his cheek, every fiber of his being craves more. It's all he can do to stay still, trying to count the remaining ceiling beams through the darkness.

Eventually, the exhaustion of the day and the comfortable heat of Arthur's aura take their toll. Shae's nerves ease, and he finds himself drifting to sleep. He isn't cold at all. He could get used to this.

☽○☾

SHAE WAKES THE next morning, even warmer and more comfortable than when he fell asleep, and knows immediately that something has gone terribly wrong.

When he fell asleep, he was next to Arthur. Now, he is very much *on top of* Arthur. Cheek and hand pressed against his broad chest, one of his legs actually hooked over one of Arthur's. His heartbeat picks up, and he can't help flinching away.

Trying to, at least. At the slight movement, Arthur's arm tightens around his waist, pinning him in place. Shae can't crane his head up enough to see Arthur's face, but he has to still be asleep. Clear dawn light creeps into the ruined room, illuminating Arthur's stubbled jaw, the lines of his throat. His chest rises and falls gently, steadily, and Shae moves with it as if Arthur's breath is a tide, ebbing and flowing through him.

Shae can barely feel the cold darkness seated beside his heart. He feels strong enough to move mountains, to raise an army, to rip out Izen's spine with a single word. Strong enough to do anything except extricate himself from Arthur's comfortable embrace. He's never felt this comfortable in his life, heat coursing down his body and pooling below his stomach.

Oh, fuck.

Shae's eyes fly wide open as he realizes how hard he is. His cock might be trapped snug in his trousers, but it's very definitely pressed against Arthur's hip.

With new strength born of panic, Shae wriggles out from under Arthur's arm. The paladin grumbles something in his sleep, then blinks open his eyes. "Morning." His voice is raspy with sleep in a way that shoots straight down to Shae's cock. "Everything all right?"

"Everything's fine!" Shae says, jumping to his feet. "Just going out for a minute." He flees the broken temple before Arthur can say anything else. The crisp morning air is like a bucket of cold water, washing the worst of the panic from him, but does nothing to quell the arousal pulsing in his veins.

Duchess barely looks up at him from her thorough grazing. Shae avoids eye contact with her, as if she would recognize and judge his inappropriate feelings for her human. He leans behind the decaying wood-shed, out of sight from horse and man alike, a good fifty feet away from the main church. Tips his head against the wood and tries to catch his breath.

His cock still strains in his trousers, and he can't get Arthur's touch out of his head. It's like traces of his aura have wrapped around Shae's throat, choking him. He's never been more eager to strangle himself in desire.

Eyes fluttering shut, he slides his hand under his waistband. Not even bothering to unlace his trousers, it's a tight fit, but the friction and awkward angle are nothing compared to the remembered sensations driving him. He thinks about Arthur's hand on his chin, and imagines that same broad hand is the one stroking him now instead of his own. Would Arthur touch gently, the way he moved Shae's hands and legs when he was teaching him how to ride?

Or roughly, pinning Shae down? Covering him completely. Insistently.

Shae's too desperate to manage *gentle* right now. His hand twists tightly, and his hips rock into the friction. He's so close. He remembers Arthur's breath on his neck, the sound of his sleep-rough voice.

Shae covers his mouth to muffle his moan as he spills onto his fingers.

The pleasure ebbs from his body, and clarity washes in. Shae grimaces and withdraws his hand, weighing the options before wiping his seed on the grass at his feet. Then he closes his eyes and meditates, clearing his mind of everything but the morning breeze in his hair, until his breathing steadies and there's a chance his face isn't bright red anymore, before he heads back for breakfast.

ARTHUR

They stop at Hannick after leaving the temple. The village is small and quiet, and most of the occupants are out farming or fishing, but there are a couple of small shops, and Arthur and Shae could use some more supplies.

Shae agrees to the stop with barely a word. He hasn't spoken to Arthur all morning, closed off and distracted by something.

Passing through the quiet streets, Arthur and Shae stick out like blazing torches. Arthur's used to being stared at in uniform, but he's not used to the way people's faces change when their gazes slide from him to the skinny necromancer at his side. He wonders if that's the expression that crossed *his* face, the first night he saw Shae. He remembers his instinctive revulsion.

No wonder Shae's prickly.

Shae stops when they reach the town square, a wide-open block crowned by a rippling fountain. "I'll stay out here while you get what we need," he says, glancing at the fountain, the shop banners, anywhere but at Arthur. He's been avoiding eye contact all morning.

Maybe he's mad that Arthur somehow grabbed him in the middle of the night. Or maybe he's mad about having to tell Arthur about the whole touch thing in the first place. Arthur doesn't feel guilty about dragging answers from him, but he feels a little guilty about how much he enjoyed waking up with Shae curled up against him.

This is supposed to be a business arrangement. Don't read too much into it, Arthur.

"All right." Arthur hands the reins over to Shae. "Duchess, be good for Shae, okay?"

The mare nudges into his hand when he pets her one last time before heading into the general store.

He buys most of what they need easily enough, then chats with the shopkeeper as she sorts through everything. "Have you had any problems with wild animals lately? I ran across some odd tracks on my way in."

"Three and a half silver," the woman says. "And no trouble I've heard of. Is that what the lot of you are after, wild animals?"

Arthur counts the coins onto the counter. "What do you mean?"

"You aren't with the other group?" She recounts the coins very slowly. "Hell of a coincidence, then. We had a whole troop of paladins riding through just a week ago, ten or twelve of them."

Arthur frowns. "Were they Varans? With the sun—"

"Same sun on their tunics as yours, yes, I know Varans from Sephinians."

"What were they doing in the area?"

"No idea. They didn't stop at all, just rode right through." She pushes his purchases back over the counter. "Anything else I can do for you?"

Arthur's about to say no, he's good, when a display in the corner catches his eye. A glass-fronted cabinet of jewelry and other precious objects. Bottles, candlesticks, a knife crusted with red gems in the hilt. "Actually, maybe. What's in here?"

The woman steps around the counter to join him at the cabinet. "There's a lock spell on it, don't touch it yourself. None of these are enchanted, but they're all enchantment quality." She grins. "Or they're just pretty, if you're not a mage of any sort."

"Are you a mage yourself?"

"No, not me, I'm just here to take their coin. See anything you like? That dagger might do well with your sunshine magic."

But Arthur's not looking at the dagger. His eyes catch on a row of rings. "Can I get a closer look at these?"

The shopkeeper unlatches the cabinet and lays the rings out on the counter for him to look at. There are ten, and most are gold with small gems, but a few are silver. There's one in particular he can't help thinking would suit the rings Shae already wears. A silver band set with a small, round-cut golden topaz. He's pretty sure it would fit Shae's delicate hand.

"How much for this one?"

"Twenty gold." She grins slyly at him. "And you'll make the lucky lady or gentleman very happy, I'm sure. Special occasion?"

"No occasion," Arthur says, reaching for his coin purse again. "But I'll take it."

He hands over everything Shae's paid him so far plus a fair amount more, then exits with the ring in a velvet bag, tucked hidden in the inside pocket of his belt pouch.

Lost in thought, Arthur returns to Shae and Duchess. He's not sure why he bought the ring, other than that it would look pretty on Shae's hand, perhaps winning him a smile for the effort. Maybe Arthur's self-restraint has been shaken by news of other paladins riding through. He feels unsettled. Distracted in too many directions at once. Like he should be thinking more about Shae than the order, but more about the order than Shae.

The Radiant Order is headquartered in Ostaris, the capital city of Charain, and most of their force remains in that area, in defense of the Bright Cathedral. The western border with Praia is far more volatile than the northern one; after all, Lyrisenia is less a state than a scattered collection of settlements nobody *wants* to conquer. Too little soil and too many demons for profitable farming, and the Northern Barrier keeps the worst of those demons on the Lyrisenian side of the border.

Two or three paladins might be sent up north if a local church requested their aid, but ten or twelve? There's something big happening, and something in Arthur aches for not knowing. A year ago, he might have been in that troop, riding with his brothers and sisters under the Radiant banner. Now, he's alone, with just his horse and a pretty necromancer who might be ignoring him.

Shae's head is down, intent on scratching Duchess's neck as she pats him down for treats, but he looks up as soon as Arthur gets within twenty feet. Then down again, apparently unwilling to make eye contact after the reflexive movement.

"Did you get everything?" he asks.

"We're good to go," Arthur answers, taking the reins back from Shae.

Shae grimaces and twists the ring on his forefinger. "Great. Let's get out of this place." He's in a dark mood again.

Arthur considers pulling out the ring in an attempt to cheer him up, but decides to leave it for now. It's probably a bad time to give Shae a gift if he doesn't want it thrown back in his face.

)O(

ARTHUR HOPED SHAE'S mood would improve after they left Hannick and its staring inhabitants, but that hope proves futile as the day wears on. Shae continues avoiding eye contact and conversation, just as deliberately as the time Arthur dared ask his age.

A few days ago, Arthur would have chalked it up to Shae's unreasonable prickly temperament. Now, though, he's starting to figure out that Shae's prickliness is more a defense mechanism than anything else. The necromancer does everything for a reason, even if Arthur might not understand what that reason is.

So, when they stop to water Duchess at a sandy bank of the Rising Run, Arthur asks straight-out, "Are you pissed off at me?"

Predictably, Shae responds by turning his head away, looking out over the sunlit waters. "No."

"Then why have you been avoiding me all day?"

Shae fiddles with one of his rings again. "I thought you could probably use some space, after, well. I was really clingy last night, and I know that can be annoying."

Arthur frowns. "Have people told you that in the past?"

"Not in so many words, but I'm not an idiot."

Arthur's not an idiot either, and he recognizes the possessiveness surging up in him. He hates the idea of Shae cuddling up to past unknown swords for hire. But he hates the idea of Shae being shoved aside even more.

He reaches out and touches Shae's chin, and he barely has to press his fingers to turn Shae towards him, like a flower turning towards the sun. "I don't mind the clingy thing," Arthur says, because all right, maybe he is an idiot. "You don't have to worry about that with me."

"You say that now," Shae says darkly, but he blushes as he says it, and Arthur's heart flips in his chest.

SHAE

They run across the body three mornings later. Duchess notices it first; her ears prick suddenly forward, and her neck arches. Arthur places a hand on her shoulder and draws her to a halt. "I don't sense anything," he says quietly. "Do you?"

"No." Shae's rings are no colder than usual on his fingers. Then he sees it, a depression in the foliage on the roadside ahead, and a flash of green cloth. He points. "Wait, there's something there."

Arthur passes Duchess's reins to him wordlessly, draws his sword, and stalks forward. Shae holds the reins tightly, hoping Duchess can't tell how unnerved he is. He likes her a lot, but she's still gigantic, and he doesn't think he can keep hold of her if she panics.

A few moments later, Arthur swears and sheathes his sword. "He's dead," he calls over to Shae.

Shae swears too and leads Duchess over.

For all his association with the dead over the past ten years, he only rarely encounters the *recently* dead. He's used to skeletons, dried-out corpses, shells that only echo the people they once held. He's not used to this: a man slumped sideways in the underbrush, utterly motionless. Hardly even a smell fouling the fresh country air. If they move him, his limbs will be stiff. There will be discoloration. But until they disturb him, he could just be asleep.

Shae's vision swims. For a second, he sees his father's body, slumped in their little front yard. Arms up, drenched in blood. Shae blinks, and he's back in the present. There's no blood on this body. No sign of any injury at all.

Arthur crouches and turns the dead man onto his back. The body's tall, middle-aged, with a heavy beard. His eyes are still open. "He was a hunter, judging by his clothes," Arthur says. "He didn't even draw his knife."

"I don't think he just had a heart attack," Shae says.

"Neither do I." Arthur stands up, grimacing. He gestures down the road. "That must be his pack on the ground. He dropped it and ran—but what was he running from? A bandit would have taken the pack. An animal would have taken him. Something isn't right."

Something isn't right. Shae can see that clearly. "I could ask him what happened."

Arthur whips around. "What do you mean by that?"

Shae bites his lip. "I can reanimate him for a minute and ask how he died."

"Absolutely not." Arthur moves closer, standing between him and the body. "I told you I'd help with anything not counter to my oath, but raising the dead is a few fucking miles across the line."

"It's not raising the dead," Shae snaps, then takes a shuddering breath, forcing himself to calm down. "I won't touch his soul. That—that's cruel, and it doesn't end well."

"Do you know that from experience?" Duchess dances beside them, and Shae flinches back from the movement. Arthur takes the reins from him and runs a soothing hand down her neck. "Sorry," Arthur continues, and Shae's not sure which of them he's talking to. "Just tell me, how is *reanimating* the dead different from *raising* the dead?"

Another deep breath, before Shae snaps again. Arthur's questions are reasonable, even if they drag up moments Shae prefers to forget. "I'd just be waking up his body and relying on the body's last memories. What his eyes saw, what his ears heard. It won't be *him*, with any personality or emotions. Just the body's record of his last moments."

Arthur's still frowning, but he says, "All right."

Shae doesn't quite register the agreement at first. He blinks. "What?"

"All right," Arthur repeats. His frown melts into a lopsided grin, lighting up his golden face. "I trust you on this. And I really want to know what happened. I don't think it's a coincidence that we found this guy."

"I don't think so either," Shae says, a little breathlessly. Gods, Arthur's going to kill him if he keeps saying crazy things like *I trust you on this.*

Arthur tethers Duchess across the road, and Shae fetches the man's fallen pack. There's nothing inside but food, water, and a net trap. Almost certainly a local hunter, but nothing to identify him. As Shae walks there and back, he looks at the ground. There's a clear track from the man running, but nothing else obvious in the hard-packed dirt.

Shae kneels at the man's side and reaches out, but stops before touching him. This will hurt—the necromancy always hurts now, like Shae has less and less of himself to give each time. But maybe it will hurt a little less if he trusts Arthur too.

"I'm going to touch his chest and restart his heart and lungs enough for him to talk to us," Shae explains. "He'll probably gasp and choke at first. It's disturbing, but it doesn't last long."

"Good to know," Arthur says. "Should I do anything?"

Shae twists his rings around. "Could you hold onto me while I do it? The contact will help."

"All right." Arthur crouches down behind him.

Shae expects a hand on his shoulder. Maybe on his back. Instead, there's a gentle touch as Arthur brushes the hair from the back of his neck, then settles his bare palm flush against Shae's vertebrae. Heat floods through him, and he bites his lip on a moan of relief.

"Like this?" Arthur asks, so close his breath stirs in Shae's hair.

"That's great," Shae manages. "Really great." He takes a deep breath to steady his nerves, then presses his own palm against the center of the dead man's chest.

The body is cold, even through layers of leather and wool. Shae closes his eyes and calls on the cold within him. It answers eagerly, running down his arm, piercing bloodlessly through the dead hunter.

Shae feels the cold as always, but it doesn't consume him. Arthur's hand on his neck grounds him in life as he reaches for death.

"Wake blood and breath," he whispers in Lyrisenian. "Give me your voice. Give me your time."

The last word hasn't left his lips when the body seizes up, a horrible gurgling sound rising from his throat. The mouth opens, and spit flies into the dark beard. His eyes don't move, still dead and sightless, but when the convulsion ends, the faint rise and fall of breath remains.

"Radiant Vara," Arthur whispers behind Shae's ear. His hand is tense on Shae's neck.

"We have about a minute." Shae's slightly dizzy, but far stronger than he would be without Arthur at his back. He says, louder, "What were you doing just now, friend?"

Wet breath rattles through the body's throat. Words come with it, rumbling echoes of a deep, strong voice: "I was running. I was heading home, and then I was running."

"Where is home?"

"I don't know," the hunter says. He doesn't sound lost, just matter of fact.

The smell is overpowering. Shae resists the urge to cover his nose, even if the dead body wouldn't know he was being rude. "What were you running from?"

"I don't know," the hunter says again.

Either he doesn't remember, or he couldn't identify the threat. Shae considers his questions carefully. "Did you see it?"

"Yes." The ribcage heaves. "There were two."

"What did they look like?"

"A shadow. Not an animal, not real. Too many teeth. Too many eyes." The hunter's entire body twitches with some remembered reflex. "There was a dead man with it."

Shae's heartbeat picks up. He wonders if Arthur can feel his pulse where they touch. "Was he walking?" he asks quickly. "What color were his eyes?"

"Yes," the hunter answers. "Red."

Arthur's hand tenses again on Shae's neck. Shae swallows, but keeps going with the questions, not wanting to waste any time. "What happened then?"

"I fell," the dead man sighs, lips barely moving. "Then everything was cold and dark."

Shae frowns. "What's the last thing you saw?"

"Nothing," the dead man says. "I saw nothing." His voice grows fainter as he speaks, and his ribcage shudders weakly under Shae's hand.

"Did it hurt?" Shae asks quickly. "Did you feel anything?"

But with one final rattle, the dead man slumps motionless once more. The flow of cold power cuts off, the last of it recoiling up Shae's arm. Shae hangs his head, counting his breaths as his power resettles beneath his heart. It's easier than it's ever been before, with Arthur's thumb gently stroking the side of his neck, easing away the tension.

"Thanks," Shae says eventually, and immediately regrets it because Arthur lets go and stands up.

"Red eyes," Arthur says, shaking his head. "Either demon possession or an acolyte of the Flame Twins, and I wouldn't bet on the latter."

"I wouldn't either." Shae twists one of his rings, his nervousness mounting once again.

They're still so far away from the border, surely Izen can't reach this far south yet. The spells in Shae's rings are still intact, surely Izen can't have found him on purpose. It could be another demon, with another target.

"And the other creature sounds like another vaidkos," Arthur says. "I don't like that we've run across two of them now. That's as many as I've ever seen in my life, within one week. But he didn't say anything about it attacking him, and I don't see any injuries on him."

Shae stands up too. His shakiness and nausea have nothing to do with the after-effects of magic. "It's the same as the one in the graveyard," he says quietly. "It took his soul."

The warm breeze rustles through the trees, stirring up road dust and whipping Shae's coat around him. Arthur puts a hand to his chest in warding. "Light guide us," he mutters. "I need to report this to the order."

Reflexive fear tightens Shae's nerves. He can't afford too long of a delay, and the thought of Arthur leaving him for the Radiant Order makes his pulse pick up. "Are any of you stationed nearby?"

"No, but the next village should be close. I'll just talk to the local guard and pass a message along," Arthur answers, alleviating Shae's sudden worry. He rubs his stubbled jaw, looking down at the hunter. Then he kneels down and gently closes the dead man's eyes. "We'll need to tell them to come out and retrieve our friend anyway."

"All right."

Shae's more relieved than he should be that Arthur doesn't want to detour. He's gotten far too used to being able to rely on his companion, instead of keeping him at arms' length, no closer and no farther. And Shae has a sinking feeling that all of this—the soul stealing, Izen, his own weakening spirit—is related. He's going to need all the help he can get.

The sand is pouring through the hourglass. Shae doesn't know how much is left. It might be time to tell Arthur the truth about his journey. The whole truth.

ARTHUR

They don't stay long in the next town, putting in a good afternoon's travel after reporting the hunter's body to the local guard. As the evening deepens, they make camp in a dry cave. Other travelers have used it before, judging from the footprints and campfire remnants, but nobody recently enough for Arthur to expect company. He makes sure Duchess has food and water, then walks a loop around the entrance and says the prayer to set the warding magic. Same as every night.

Except when he's done, he opens his eyes to see Shae leaning against the cave entrance, watching him. Arthur mostly doesn't find the necromancer unnerving anymore, but there's an odd, contemplative stillness to his dark gaze now. Arthur feels like he's under inspection.

He's not sure he dislikes it.

"What are the parameters of your warding spell?" Shae asks.

Arthur answers as he steps out of the cave again, looking for enough dry wood to start a fire. "The boundary extends about a hundred feet past the circle I walk. If any mortal creature bigger than a rabbit crosses, or anything demonic of any size, it alerts me."

"Could they know we're here, though?"

"I suppose. I don't have cloaking magic." Radiant Vara's purview is more concerned with revelation than concealment.

"That's what I figured." Out of the corner of his eye, Arthur sees Shae move to the center of the cave. He sits down next to the dead ashes of the last traveler's fire. "I need to renew one of my cloaking rings, then. There's blood involved, so don't look if that bothers you."

He's already shrugging off his coat and rolling up his left sleeve. Arthur's stomach flips, but it's not the sight of blood that bothers him. Shae's casual disregard for his own welfare is getting frustrating.

But Arthur has no right to stop him. "At least let me build the fire first. It's getting dark."

"I work fine in the dark," Shae says. He sets his knife on the ground and waits anyway.

Arthur gets the fire going, then grabs a roll of bandages and a jar of denseed oil from his saddlebags. Shae might not care about cutting himself, but Arthur will make sure he gets patched up properly after.

When Arthur sits next to him, Shae opens his mouth like he might say something, then purses his lips. His eyes lower, long lashes kissing his cheeks, as he twists one of his rings off. The plain silver band looks cold in his gloved left palm.

He unsheathes his knife. The firelight flickers gold against the steel blade. Arthur's closer than he was the last time, and now he can see the older scars littering Shae's skin. Some look neat, intentional. Some don't.

Arthur has his own scars. Training injuries, battle wounds. Childhood mishaps. The marks on Shae's skin still bother him in a way he can't quite explain. Maybe it's that Shae hired him for protection, but Arthur isn't allowed to protect Shae from himself.

Shae cuts a neat line parallel to the scabbed-over wound from the graveyard. Blood wells up immediately, and he drops the knife to press his fingers to the cut. He murmurs something under his breath. Then he brings his red-painted fingers to the ring in his palm and says another phrase.

Cold, heavy energy fills the air. Arthur's breath hitches, and Shae shudders, biting his lip. On instinct, Arthur reaches out and grabs Shae's wrist. He thinks about sunlight, fire, summer days. He thinks about the way his heart feels when Shae smiles, and tries to guide that heat through the connection of their skin, into Shae.

The silver ring flashes bright white, then darkens to its usual hue. An ordinary silver ring, except for the red gleam of blood.

Shae's breath steadies, but he doesn't pull from Arthur's grasp. "That was—that helped a lot. Thanks."

Arthur doesn't want to let go either. He wants to keep hold of Shae's wrist, their skin heating with the contact.

He lets go anyway and grabs the denseed oil. "Did it work?"

"Yes." Shae fishes a handkerchief from the inside of his coat and starts cleaning off the ring and his fingers. When he's put the ring back on and dropped the handkerchief, he lets Arthur take his arm again and rub a drop of the slick protective oil over the cut.

The wound is shallow, and it's already stopped bleeding. Arthur winds a length of bandage around Shae's arm anyway. It's the principle of the thing. If Shae won't take care of himself, Arthur will do it for him. There's something soothing about pulling the cotton taut against Shae's scarred skin, flattening out the edges before he ties the ends together. When he's done, he feels a tension he hadn't even noticed leave his chest.

Shae shifts around to sit with his arms around his bent knees. He glances at Arthur, then at the fire, and says quietly, "I'm twenty-two."

Arthur doesn't understand at first. Then he does, and all the breath leaves his body in a sharp exhalation. The math is painfully easy. He doesn't know what to say, but that's just as well, because it seems like Shae is ready to talk.

"My parents died when I was twelve," Shae continues. His voice is calm but distant, and he keeps looking at the fire, not at Arthur. "Bandits. I wasn't ready to let go, so I followed the old legends and traveled to an ancient cathedral north of the Lyralan Crater. Mother said the cathedral belonged to the Trickster. Father said it belonged to the Songbird. Either way, there was a summoning circle I could redraw." His lips twitch in a cold smile. "Summoning the demon was easier than I expected."

Arthur leans forward, transfixed by the blank mask of Shae's face lit by fire. The light doesn't reach the necromancer's eyes.

"He taught me necromancy in exchange for staying in the mortal realm. I thought I was clever and trapped him in an array in the old cathedral, but he didn't seem to mind. He just wanted to be here. I should have been suspicious, but I was—I wasn't really sane at that point. I just wanted my parents back."

"You were twelve," Arthur says.

"I was irresponsible," Shae corrects harshly, but he's clearly not mad at Arthur. He's mad at himself, twelve years old and grieving, and Arthur's heart hurts just thinking about that. "I made the deal and then I ran, leaving him in that array. I told myself I could banish him again later, whenever I wanted. But I've been too fucking cowardly to go back, until now, when it might be too late."

Shae's brittle in the firelight. Like the dagger's blade, reflecting the flames but still cold at heart. The resentment in his voice resonates through Arthur's bones, and he remembers the day after Ronan ran away. After the healers fixed him. He'd gone back to his room, seen the bed where they'd fucked, the table where they'd shared mugs of ale, too much ale, the shirt on the floor that Ronan always liked to steal. The loss and self-loathing surged up inside him, and instead of praying, Arthur punched a hole in the wall. The pain didn't help, but he did it again, just to see.

Shae hasn't been punching walls for the past ten years. He's been too busy punching holes in himself.

"Why do you think it might be too late?" Arthur asks.

Shae's mouth twists. "The array is fading. I cast it when I was twelve, of course it wasn't going to last forever. He can't leave, or I'd know about it, but I think he's sending the vaidkos out to catch souls for him to eat. That will make him stronger. Either way, I need to banish him before the array fails completely, or I'll never catch him again." He turns to face Arthur then, and the firelight finally sets his eyes ablaze. "Banishing him will break the contract and send him back to the dark realm. I'll lose my magic. I'll be free of it."

His voice is strong as steel, no hint of fragility left, and Arthur's pulse quickens. He shifts closer, reaches, and when Shae doesn't pull away, he drapes his arm around the smaller man's shoulders.

"If anyone can do that, it's you," Arthur says.

Shae melts immediately into the embrace, head tilting onto Arthur's chest. "Maybe," he says quietly. "But I can't do it alone."

They watch the fire together. A single glow of light as the darkness grows around them. The stone walls of the cave like a starless, breathless sky over their heads. The quiet grows comfortable.

But one last question claws its way from Arthur's throat. He hates to ask, but he'll be thinking about it forever if he doesn't. "Did it work?"

Shae doesn't answer for a while. He doesn't move at all, just slumps bonelessly against Arthur's side. Eventually he says, his voice devoid of emotion, "It didn't work. I couldn't bring them back."

Arthur just holds him tighter and stares into the fire.

SHAE

All right, so that wasn't the whole truth. He chickened out at the last minute.

But it's more of the truth than Shae's told anyone in ten years, and breaking open his secrets leaves him feeling raw, his heart sliced open in a way that's difficult to bandage closed. He eats and helps clean up mechanically, quietly, and he's grateful Arthur doesn't ask anything else. As soon as he can, he goes to bed, closing his eyes to the smooth stone walls of the cave.

He drifts to sleep, exhausted from talking to Arthur and the nameless dead man, from spilling out his memories and magic and blood all day.

The cave closes around Shae, a tomb of shadows. He stands in the tomb, and dead vines grasp his ankles. Stone effigies pin back his arms. A bright white line fractures and withers into dust. He's in the Lyralan cathedral, but he's also in his family's cottage. The shape moving towards him has horns and wings, but it's also two people, and the hatred in their eyes burns just as fiercely. He doesn't want to see them. He'd rather face the demon, he's trapped by stone and death and—

Someone touches his shoulder.

Shae wakes with a pounding heart, each breath an ice-cold dagger in his lungs. He struggles, reaching for his knife or his rings or a handful of dirt. All he finds is warm skin under cotton, two hands gently but firmly catching his wrists.

"Hey, easy there." Arthur's voice is rough with sleep. Only the outline of him is visible in the faint starlight, but his aura's as warm as a summer day. "It's just me."

Shae slumps back onto the cave's dirt floor, eyes wide, still trembling. "Sorry," he whispers. "I thought…" The dream's already slipping from his mind. He can't tell if another line of the array really broke, or if he just dreamed it.

"You sounded like you were having a nightmare," Arthur says quietly. "I wasn't sure if I should wake you up or not."

Shae really doesn't want to know what he sounded like, but the embarrassment is nothing beneath the warmth blooming in his chest. Maybe it's just a job to Arthur, maybe it's just a paladin thing, but right now, it doesn't matter. Shae just likes the way Arthur acts like he cares about him.

"Thanks," he says. "I'm fine now."

Arthur lies back down next to him, and Shae misses his touch the moment his hands leave his wrists. But in the next breath, Arthur's saying, "Come here, it's cold tonight," and pulling him in.

This time, there's no mystery about their closeness. Arthur pulls, and Shae shamelessly follows, curling up against the larger man. He's fully enclosed in the heat of Arthur's arms, the steady thudding of his heartbeat, but there's no sense of entrapment. This is comfort, not a cage.

Shae feels a warm, fleeting pressure on the top of his head, so quick he might have imagined it. If it wasn't impossible, he would think it was a kiss. He's too exhausted and comfortable to think much of it.

If he dreams again, he doesn't remember by morning.

)O(

A FEW DAYS later, Arthur helps him onto Duchess's back like usual. They've fallen into a routine of casually chatting as they travel by day, and cuddling together at night. Arthur hasn't mentioned the nightmares or Shae's confession, which would be great except Shae has nothing to distract himself from the way Arthur's hands linger on his thighs, the way he smiles up at Shae, as he positions him in the saddle.

"Remember, thumbs up," Arthur says, and is physically readjusting Shae's hands really necessary?

Maybe the problem isn't the way Arthur keeps casually touching him. The problem is how much Shae likes it.

Shae squeezes his calves to make Duchess go forward, which has no effect. He kicks a little harder—he doesn't

want to hurt her, even though Arthur says he won't—
and she takes a single reluctant step forward, ears
pinned back.

"Is she mad at me?"

"You're pulling back on the reins," Arthur says.
"Relax." The gentle pat to Shae's knee is definitely not
necessary. Heat flushes up Shae's leg from the point of
contact.

Shae takes a deep breath, forcing himself to relax
with the same feat of concentration he needs to
awaken a corpse. He moves his hands forward, back
to the position Arthur originally showed him, and
kicks again. This time, the chestnut mare moves into
a walk immediately, as if the previous two attempts
hadn't even happened. Shae jerks in his seat with the
first step, and barely stops himself from clamping his
legs down to stay in place.

"Well done," Arthur says, and Shae thinks he's being
sarcastic until he looks down and sees the way Arthur
smiles up at him. The simple praise crawls into his hind-
brain and takes root there, far sweeter than it should be.

Riding is easier now. Shae's probably getting ahead of
himself, being so pleased at being able to sit the walk,
but he's getting used to the steady movement beneath
him. He doesn't have to put as much thought into just
moving with Duchess's gait, and he's able to pay more
attention to his surroundings as they set off.

They're only about a week from the border. This far
north, the lush Charaini forest gives way to darker, taller
trees, their trunks thin enough to bend with storm
winds instead of breaking, their whiplike boughs held

close together. The road is clear and mostly level, but the hills grow rockier around them. The weather's still warm, probably, though Shae can't differentiate between the weather and the warmth of Arthur's aura.

"How long have you had Duchess?" Shae asks, because he's greedy for the sound of Arthur's voice.

Arthur grins and pats the mare's glossy neck. "Five years. I've had her since the day I took my oath. She was a graduation present from some of my friends in the order. Bernard and Freya knew my family wasn't as well off as theirs were, and they took me out horse shopping as soon as the vigil was over." He laughs. "I learned not to ride her around town if I wasn't in uniform, at first. The rest of my wardrobe was so cheap, I got stopped a few times by guards who thought I'd stolen her."

Shae finds it difficult to imagine Arthur looking anything less than perfectly in place. People like Shae are the ones who get stopped by the guards, not golden boys like Arthur. The image makes his lips twitch in a smile. "They sound like good friends."

"Don't misunderstand, they're terrible troublemakers," Arthur says quickly, but he still smiles too. "But good friends, yes."

"And where's your family from?"

"Port Charain," Arthur says. "My brother's a sailor now, like Ma used to be."

He continues talking about his family, needing little prompting from Shae, and Shae settles back to listen. He used to hate hearing about parents and children, brothers and sisters, furious and heartsick thinking about his own losses. But over the years, that's faded to wistfulness. He's glad there are happy families out there.

Arthur sighs at one point, reaching out to pet Duchess again. He's looking at the road ahead, not at Shae. "I haven't spoken to them in a year, though. Not since the incident with Ronan."

"Is that the guy—your friend who stole the relic? Was your family upset about that?" Shae's not used to feeling indignant on someone else's behalf. It's one thing for the Radiant Order to punish Arthur for someone else's mistakes, but his own family turning on him? Shae's parents had at least resented him for something he'd done with his own two hands.

"They don't know about it." Arthur's next smile is hollow, and Shae almost regrets asking. "Maybe it's cowardly of me, but I wanted to wait until after my sentencing, so I could tell them whether or not it turned out okay." Shae wants to tell him it is okay, that he isn't cowardly, but he doesn't manage to pull together the words before Arthur continues. "And Ronan wasn't just a friend. We were lovers."

Shae's hands tighten instinctively on the reins, and Duchess slows until Shae forcibly relaxes. "Oh."

He's not like Arthur. He's not good at listening, and he's not good at saying the right thing. Arthur's gotten him to confess things he'd never confessed to anyone before, and it hurt but he felt safe. Now that the tables are turned, all Shae can think about is how jealous he is of a priest-killing thief.

"I'm sure your family would—"

His magic twinges within him. Seconds later, one of his rings flares cold on his right hand, sharper and more intense than he's ever felt. He chokes, the pain buckling him over in the saddle.

Arthur swears, the sound more distant than it should be, and blazing heat briefly steadies Shae—then absence. There's a tug on the saddle, and Duchess suddenly backs up. Clutching her mane for balance, Shae looks up through the pain. Panic freezes the scene around him, slowing down time.

He sees Arthur drawing his sword. The path curves sharply ahead, rocks rising tall around them, and the unmistakable malformed shape of a vaidkos stalks through the dark tree line. This one has only four legs, but four hideous vestigial wings stretch from its spine.

A flicker of movement at the edge of his vision. Another to the north. They're surrounded, and Shae's ring alerted him far too late.

"Stay back," Arthur tells him, his blade gleaming like a torch in the sunlight. Then the first vaidkos lunges for him, and they meet in a crash of steel and fang. They part, both unharmed, and circle each other a few steps before lunging together again.

Shae can't do anything besides try to stay on as Duchess dances beneath him. His heart pounds in his throat. He feels sickeningly helpless. Vaidkos aren't dead. His power has no control over them, and that's part of why he hired a sword in the first place. This is why Arthur's here.

But it's different actually seeing Arthur in danger.

The second vaidkos barrels from the trees.

"Look out!" Shae yells on instinct, and Arthur barely dances out of the creature's way. Both vaidkos fix their many-eyed gazes on Arthur. They're more intelligent than mundane animals. They know the man with the sword is the true threat, and they'll take him down before turning on Shae.

"Ride back to the last crossroads," Arthur calls hoarsely. He swings his sword, fending off another blow. "I'll meet you there."

"I'm not leaving," Shae snaps.

Even if he wanted to, he's not sure he could control Duchess in such a state. She flinches back a few steps, knocking Shae sideways in the saddle. Her ears flick from monster to monster, and Shae can feel the instinctive, primal fear shivering through her body.

But she hasn't abandoned her master, and Shae won't either.

He can't do anything while he's trying—badly—not to fall off a horse. He leans forward and swings his leg around to dismount before he falls. But his previous dismounts didn't involve another monster crashing through the trees right next to them. Duchess shies away as he moves, and he falls the rest of the way to the ground. He drops to one knee, scrambling backwards, out of the way of the mare's hooves.

His new bruises and scrapes barely register. All his attention is focused on Arthur, dancing like a golden flame between leaping shadows. The paladin moves as if his blade is an extension of his body. The golden streaks through the air aren't an illusion of sunlight and dust; they're magic sharpening his sword, shielding his back.

But there are three vaidkos. No, there are four. And Arthur is only one man.

Shae rips off his glove and pulls out his knife.

There's no time for careful, deliberate cuts. He slices the blade down his palm and slams his hand to the ground, willing the blood out into the dirt. They're a day out from the nearest town, and there are no graveyards nearby. There's just the forest, the constant turnover of life and death. The lingering, ambient echoes of mortality. If he reaches for it, spends enough of his strength, maybe—

Black smoke billows before him with a crack of thunder. Shae falls backwards with the sudden displacement of air. The impact is jarring, and his bloodied palm scrapes against the hard dirt road. He thinks for a second that his magic has gone wrong, except he hasn't even started yet. The spell fizzles out, unspent.

The smoke coalesces into a shadow standing above him, and a pair of rotted leather boots before his eyes. Mouth gone dry, Shae looks up into blood-red eyes in a dead white face.

The man's skin is warped and sagging. Like it spent a week in the river, then a week out of it. His hair is little more than tangles of mud and leaves, dried and flaking. The red eyes are the only part of him that looks alive, glittering as they fix on Shae.

"Little Shaesarenna," Izen rasps through the dead man's lips. "I didn't expect to see you here."

Shae's skin crawls at the almost-familiar voice. He lunges for his knife, expecting a blow of magic at any moment, hoping his jewelry can protect him long enough to let him fight back. But Izen doesn't strike. He stands utterly still, surrounded by wisps of red and black smoke, as Shae scrambles to his feet.

"If you aren't here for me, then why are you here?" he asks, his voice high with nerves.

Izen tilts his head, and the dead man's face doesn't move, but Shae can *see* the way the demon's true face would smirk, eyebrows raised. "You've always thought everything was about you, Shaesarenna. Do you think I've been pining in my tower for you all these years?" His laugh is grating, broken. "I'm here for breakfast, of course."

Shae follows his gaze down the road, where Arthur faces off against the vaidkos in a clash of steel and sunlight. Arthur, with his divine aura and brilliant soul. Fear spikes through Shae's lungs, and his hand tightens around his knife hilt.

All he wants to do is run, but he's not letting Izen hurt Arthur. He's not.

"I'm impressed to see you this deep into Charain," Shae says, steadier now. "Do you need souls to break the array? It would be easier just to ask me, wouldn't it?"

Izen jerks the dead man's body around again, and his red stare sweeps up and down Shae's body. The warped face is difficult to read, but Shae thinks he sees something like interest.

"Bold as ever, my precocious little student," Izen says. "Or have you just grown tired of the cold? You had your chance to work with me before."

"That was then." Shae raises his hand to his side and drops the knife. He forces himself to look at Izen and only Izen as he walks closer. It's a bad gamble, but Izen doesn't stop him. Doesn't move aside as Shae spreads his bare, bloody palm against the dead man's chest. The smell of death and the dust and blood are enough to choke on. Shae takes a deep breath. "This is now."

And with all the strength he has, he pulls the dark power from the corpse. By the time Izen realizes what he's doing, it's too late. All the power rushes into Shae, an ice-cold torrent of dark magic, until there's nothing left for the demon to hold onto. The red light winks out of the dead man's eyes, and the body shakes apart beneath Shae's hand, cracking and crumbling into ash. A plume of smoke arcs away into the sky.

Izen's escaping, but Shae can only think about Arthur. Dizzy with magic, every nerve in his body buzzing, he channels the power and sends it forth.

ARTHUR

Arthur's sword rips through one vaidkos's throat in a spray of light and blood. Moments later, the corpse bursts into ash. Arthur darts back, circling with the other three, trying to focus on all of them at once. Sweat stings at the corners of his eyes. So far, they've only scratched him, and he's got a hell of a bruise forming on his left shoulder, but the math is simple. There's one of him, and three left of them. He's not liking his odds.

Smoke and thunder clash down the road. Arthur takes advantage of the distraction to lunge for the nearest vaidkos, but it dodges his blade just in time. He pulls back and chances a glance beyond the malformed heads.

As the smoke clears, an unfamiliar figure stands with Shae.

Before Arthur can do anything about that, two vaidkos leap at him together, and he whirls around them only to collide with the third. His magic flares, blunting the razor-sharp claws. He is the Radiant's sword, and the Radiant is his shield. The vaidkos chokes on his blade, green-black blood bubbling from his jaws, and falls to its death throes in the clouds of dust.

Only two remain, but Arthur only has a few more moments of full power left.

"Sacred Vara," he says between gasps, "your servant prays for brightest light."

His answer comes not in light, but in a scream and an explosion of darkness. Ribbons of shadow burst from the ground, whipping through the battlefield. Arthur yells, trying to dodge, trying to keep his sword clear—

But the shadows arc around him and pierce through the vaidkos instead. Their screams tear the sky as the shadows rend their flesh asunder, scales and fur and feathers flying. Bone cracks through skin and withers away, until everything is ash and silence.

The shadow ribbons vanish in the sunlight, as if they never were.

Arthur turns around, sword arm aching and heart still pounding, to see Shae staggering to his feet with Duchess a good twenty paces behind him. Shae's too far away for Arthur to make out his expression, and then he's moving too fast. The slim figure sprints towards him.

Every bone in Arthur's body wants to run towards him too, but he's still too stunned. All he can do is stand there while Shae crashes into him, grabbing his shoulders, touching his arms. His hands come away bloody. "You're all right," Shae says, and Arthur can't tell which one of them he's trying to reassure. "Are you all right? You're alive. Fuck, I thought. Fuck."

Arthur's sword falls from his hand, thumping onto the dirt road. He needs both hands to touch Shae's face, tilt him up. Shae's lips are blue, and he's cold to the touch. Arthur tries to brush a streak of dirt from his cheek and only makes it worse.

"Are you hurt?" Shae's eyes are wide and red-rimmed. "Fuck, Arthur, say something."

Arthur doesn't have words for the emotion rising inside him. He slides his hand into Shae's hair, holds him in place, and kisses his blue lips.

Shae gasps into his mouth, then kisses back.

Clumsily, desperately, too much tongue and teeth. The sweetest kiss Arthur's ever had. The adrenaline of the fight twists to arousal. He holds Shae by the hair and waist, fingers tightening, as if Shae might vanish into shadows if he let go.

Shae clutches his tunic. His neck. Holds him just as hard.

Arthur breaks away, panting for breath, and presses his forehead against Shae's. "I'm fine," he says, a grin coloring his voice. "Thanks for asking."

"Oh," Shae says, in a shocked, breathless voice that Arthur finds incredibly flattering. His gray eyes are wide. "That's good."

Arthur tries and fails again to rub the dirt from his cheek. "Can I kiss you again?"

Shae answers by leaning up into another kiss. Just as artless, just as messy. Every gasp and movement sends heat pulsing down to Arthur's cock. He groans and pulls back enough to kiss the corner of Shae's mouth, to slow this down, to savor it.

His hand brushes the rings in Shae's ear. Once, he might have recoiled at the reminder of the necromancer's art. Now, all he can think about is how much he wants the man.

Shae's hand slips against his neck, and Arthur feels Shae's flinch of pain. The wetness trickling down his skin from Shae's touch. Arthur pulls away again, as much as he wants to continue, and grabs Shae's wrist. A long, shallow cut crosses his palm, still bleeding.

"What happened?" Arthur suddenly remembers the other figure. "Who was that?"

Shae's hand trembles in his, and he tries to pull away. "It was Izen."

Arthur tightens his grip. His every instinct screams to keep Shae close, to keep him safe. To protect him better. He should have been closer. He should have been between Shae and the demon.

"I drove him off, it's fine," Shae says. He takes a deep breath and exhales in a laugh. A strange smile spreads across his face, and his voice grows stronger. "It's actually fine. We're so far from the array, his hold on the body was weak. Gods, I've spent so long hiding from him, but now all I can think about is…"

Arthur still doesn't want to let go, but the surge of fear and guilt ebbs from his lungs. He laughs too, feeling almost giddy, and kisses the tips of Shae's fingers. Watches the flush spread across Shae's cheeks.

Shae's covered in dirt and splattered in blood, clothes torn and hair disheveled. He looks about as wrecked as Arthur feels. But his lips are pink instead of blue, and his eyes are bright. He presses against Arthur from chest to thigh, and Arthur can feel his arousal hot against his.

If Shae weren't injured, Arthur would be sorely tempted to take him right here in the middle of the road, in the bloody, ash-strewn dirt. The blood on Shae's hand and the need to bandage him up are the only things propping up Arthur's sense of restraint.

"We really should get off the road," Arthur says, but instead of moving, he runs his hand up and down Shae's back. Rubs his thumb along Shae's wrist. Blood and dirt slide between their skin.

Shae's the one who has to pull away, drifting to where Duchess is now calmly grazing. Arthur takes a deep breath, grabs his sword, and follows.

☾○☽

THEY MAKE A brief camp between a dark, lush hillside and a narrow stream Arthur doesn't know the name of. He walks his warding spell with the last of his energy for the day, then kneels at the riverbank to help Shae bandage his hand.

"This would be faster if you didn't help," Shae says breathlessly as Arthur kisses his jaw. But he's the one who turns his head so their lips meet instead.

Arthur has to start over twice. He keeps fumbling the final loop of the bandage as Shae's free hand wanders his body, touching his face and shoulders and chest.

As if now that he has permission to touch Arthur, he's never going to stop. Arthur doesn't mind at all.

Finally, the bandage around his hand the only clean thing on either of them, Shae runs his fingers down the center of Arthur's chest. "Are you hurt anywhere? You never said."

"Just bruises."

Shae stands up, leaving Arthur cold and wanting. "That's good. I think it's my turn to cook—are you hungry?"

Arthur jumps up too and stops him. It's easy. The lightest touch on his shoulder has Shae turning towards him like a moth drawn to a flame. "Ravenous," Arthur says, pushing Shae against the nearest tree. He kisses the whimper from Shae's lips.

When he pulls away, Shae is dark-eyed and dazed. He licks his lips, and Arthur's attention focuses in on the brief movement of his tongue. It's barely afternoon, and the flush is clear across his cheeks as he confesses, "I have no idea what I'm doing here."

Arthur's almost ashamed of how hard that makes him. He likes the thought of being Shae's first, with a powerful possessiveness that takes him by surprise. He's never felt this way about anyone else before.

"Have you kissed anyone before?" he asks, running his thumb over Shae's lip.

Shae's eyes dart away. "What kind of idiot would kiss a necromancer?"

"In my defense," Arthur says, "you're a very attractive necromancer."

"Definitely an idiot," Shae says. But he moans into the next kiss, arching deliciously against Arthur's body, until they're both red-faced and panting. When they break apart, Shae breathes, "I want more."

Arthur swears and buries his face into Shae's neck, inhales the raw scent of him. He wants to rush into this, turn Shae around and bury himself inside with only spit between them. Overwhelm them both. He also wants to linger. Take his time. Show Shae just how incredible touching someone can be. That it's more than magic and survival.

The second impulse wins, and Arthur kisses the edge of Shae's jaw. "I want to suck your cock," he murmurs into Shae's heated skin. "Is that all right with you?"

By Shae's sharp inhale and the jerk of his body, that's definitely a yes.

SHAE

Shae barely breathes as Arthur sinks to his knees in front of him. He always thought that once he got rid of his powers, he could try to seek out ordinary things. Friendship. Sex. When he was an ordinary man without silver in his ears and grave dirt under his nails, without winter in his heart.

But Arthur wants him already, as twisted as he is. Arthur grins up at him so wickedly that Shae can forget for a moment that he's the monster here.

Careful fingers unlace Shae's trousers, brushing his cock through the fabric, and his legs threaten to buckle. He's very glad of the tree supporting him. His hands fall to Arthur's head, then his shoulders, then away.

"You can grab my hair if you want," Arthur says, leaning his cheek against Shae's thigh. One of his hands slides from Shae's hip up under his shirt and traces the line of his waistband. Shae flinches at the delicate touch, already close to the edge.

Arthur mouths his cock through his trousers, *breathes* through the fabric, and Shae bites his lip on a moan. He can't help rocking his hips against Arthur's face, and Arthur groans in response, like he's just as turned on by this as Shae is. Arthur's lips reach the head of his cock, sucking faintly through the fabric. Shae's eyes roll back at the sensation.

He's certain he's going to come before his trousers even come off, but Arthur pulls away just before he loses himself. He strokes Shae's thighs and hips with the same hands that wield both sword and sunlight with brutal strength, the same hands that gently bandage Shae's injuries. Now, Arthur uses them to take Shae apart, leaving only instinct and desire.

"How're you doing?" Arthur asks, and he has every right to look that smug.

Shae's breath hitches. "Doing fine."

"Fine," Arthur repeats, laughing. The corners of his eyes crinkle. "Yeah. Lovely weather we're having, huh?"

It could be a hurricane and Shae wouldn't care, because Arthur's pulling his trousers down his thighs and wrapping a broad, strong hand around his cock. Shae curves over with the pleasure and friction, swearing when Arthur's thumb slides over his leaking slit. He can't even tell if he's swearing in Charaini or Lyrisenian. There aren't words in either language to describe how good this feels. Not just the touch, but the aura consuming him.

Arthur's other hand slides up, shoving Shae's shirt to his waist. Fingers splay against his stomach, not holding him down, just touching him. Anchoring Shae to earth even as Arthur's other hand drives him into the tempest.

Shae's never been exposed to someone else like this, his cock hard and red against his pale stomach and dark curls, but somehow, he doesn't feel afraid or nervous. Arthur knows what he is, but still wants him.

He touches Arthur's hair again with his gloved right hand. When Arthur doesn't stop him, he pulls the wave of golden hair back so he can see better. Arthur's flushed under the dirt and stubble. There's still blood on his face. The intensity in his green eyes flays Shae open.

Arthur licks the base of his cock. Kisses a line up the shaft, then sucks his head again. The wet heat of Arthur's lips is a thousand times more intense without fabric between them. Arthur's tongue flattens over Shae's slit, and Shae can't bite back his groan of pleasure.

His hand tightens instinctively in Arthur's hair, and Arthur moans around Shae's cock. He sinks halfway down his shaft. Up again. Down. His hand pumps in time with the movement of his mouth, covering the parts of Shae he isn't swallowing. It's so fast compared to the teasing before. Shae braces himself with his bandaged hand against the tree, not caring about the pressure on his injury, fully enthralled with the sensation of Arthur bobbing his head over his cock. His hips thrust forward, and Arthur's hand pushes down on his stomach, holding him in place.

The sight is almost better than the sensation. Arthur's lips are red around his cock, his eyes lowered in concentration. Even on his knees, he's overwhelming.

"Gods," Shae pants. "*Arthur.* I'm close, if you—"

Arthur's gaze flicks up at him. He sucks down hard, and bright white magic flares around the hand on Shae's stomach. The energy blazes through them, lighting Shae's every nerve with impossible pleasure. Gasping, he jerks forward and comes into Arthur's mouth.

Pleasure and magic still race through him, tingling from the tips of his fingers to his toes, as Arthur pulls off of him and rises to his feet. He conscientiously pulls Shae's trousers back up and tucks his cock away. His hair is a mess, his lips are red, and he's clearly incredibly pleased with himself. Despite doing all the real work, he doesn't look half as exhausted as Shae feels.

Heart still pounding, Shae winds his arms around Arthur's shoulders and pulls him in so he can taste himself on Arthur's lips.

Arthur's own untouched erection presses against his hip. Shae should probably do something about that, he thinks dazedly, even though there's no way he could be anywhere near as good at this. But right now, he feels on top of the world. He can try anything.

He murmurs against Arthur's lips, "Can I blow you too?"

"I want to just keep kissing you," Arthur murmurs back, like a confession. "But I wouldn't say no to your hand. Come here."

Shae follows him to a patch of grass and winds up straddling Arthur's lap, groin pressed to Arthur's hard cock. His hands brace on Arthur's chest, then slide down.

Unbuckling Arthur's belt and unlacing his trousers is a feat in itself, with the way Arthur seems hell-bent on distracting him. Shae keeps losing focus, but he eventually gets Arthur's clothes out of the way enough to draw out the man's cock. It's just as thick as it felt through his clothes, already slick with precome.

The angle's awkward as Shae wraps his hand around it, feeling too hesitant and too forward all at once. But if he's doing this wrong, Arthur doesn't seem to care—he groans, jerking into Shae's hand, and seizes Shae's head to draw him into another kiss.

They barely part for air as Shae strokes Arthur's cock. Arthur's fingers tighten in his hair, and every once in a while Shae's scalp stings, but the edge of pain just makes the kiss all the sweeter. He wants to devour every groan Arthur makes, wants to feel every shudder through their bodies.

He doesn't realize Arthur's about to come at first, until Arthur makes a brand-new, strangled groan against his lips, and spills. Shae breaks the kiss to watch the last pulse of seed shooting over his fingers.

Looking up, he finds Arthur staring at him. That smug expression from earlier is gone, replaced with something so soft and gentle that Shae doesn't believe his eyes. He wants to, though.

"We should clean up," Shae says eventually. They're absolutely filthy, and he should probably rewrap his injured hand.

"Definitely," Arthur agrees.

But instead of getting up, he pulls Shae down to the grass with him. Shae curls up under his arm. The cool grass tickles through his clothes, and the breeze from the river soothes the flush from his neck. They fit together like they were made for each other, and Shae could get addicted to this man's touch. He closes his eyes and savors the warmth.

)O(

BY THE TIME they get up, it's too late in the evening to travel farther. Arthur takes care of Duchess while Shae awkwardly makes dinner with a hand and a half and spends the whole time thinking about Arthur's mouth.

Then he spends the entire time they eat *looking* at Arthur's mouth.

"I was distracted for a while there," Arthur says, "but I don't like that your demon and the vaidkos were able to take us by surprise."

"He's not my demon." Shae grimaces. He'd rather think about that perfect mouth around his cock, those bright green eyes staring up at him. "Unless both our magics are drastically malfunctioning, the most logical reason we didn't sense them sooner is that they weren't there sooner. They teleported in."

"Really don't like that." Arthur swigs from his water flask. His throat moves visibly as he swallows. "Radiance, it's too much of a coincidence that we've run across them this many times. Are you sure your warding's working?"

"I'm fucked if it isn't." Shae twists the ring in question. "But I actually think they were looking for you this time. I just happened to be there."

Arthur's eyebrows rise. "Me?"

"They're feeding on souls, right?" Shae gestures at him. "So, they went for the brightest soul within range."

Arthur sighs. His hair looks fire-gold under the setting sun. "We'll reach Lanwatch soon at least, and we can ask if they've had a problem with vaidkos too. Besides that, the most we can do for now is keep our guard up."

They fall into silence, and Shae resumes his surveillance of Arthur's lips until Arthur rubs his hand over his chin.

"Do I have something on my face?"

Shae jumps, nearly dropping his travel bread. He bites his lip, then says, before he can overthink his way around it, "What is this?" He waves his hand. "Us, I mean. Not the bread."

Arthur tilts his head, a familiar smug grin spreading across his face. "I was going to wait until I'd blown you again before asking," he says, uncapping his waterskin, then recapping it without drinking. "Make sure you were in a good mood. It's up to you. If you want me to just be your hired mercenary and portable fireplace, and maybe we fool around a few more times before parting ways, I can do that."

Shae has to forcibly unclench his hand from crushing the travel bread. "Is that what you want?"

"I want this to be the start of something." Arthur leans forward, focused entirely on him. "And I'm not eager to part ways that quickly."

Relief blooms through Shae as powerfully as his earlier orgasm. He ducks his head, hiding what he's sure is a stupidly happy expression. "I'm not eager to part ways either."

He's not surprised when Arthur scoots closer to him and pulls his face up. He's always doing that, drawing

Shae out of himself, forcing him to look at the world outside his shell. This time, the entire world is the kiss that Arthur drags him into.

The start of something. After ten years of endings, Shae likes the sound of that.

ARTHUR

They both rise with the dawn, tangled in each other's arms. After breakfast and before they break camp, Arthur yanks his shirt over his head and thinks he hears a muffled squeak from Shae, which is both cute and gratifying. "I'm taking a bath," he says.

"All right." Shae's eyes are clearly fixed on Arthur's abs.

Arthur takes advantage of his distraction to seize his arm. "So are you. You're filthier than I am."

"I am not." Shae gently shoves, but Arthur can tell the protest isn't sincere. He follows quickly enough, cheeks pink, to the river.

Arthur finishes stripping first and heads straight into the water so he doesn't maul Shae on the riverbank. The water is cool and clear over dark sand and pebbles. It comes to his waist at the deepest point. Overhead, a lace-like canopy of trees breaks the early sun into dappling beams of light. Arthur bends over and dunks his head in the water, scrubbing over his scalp with his fingernails. He surfaces in time to see Shae entering the water, clothes and bandages gone, fully naked except for the silver at his fingers and ears.

He's the most beautiful man Arthur's ever seen, both stronger and more fragile than he appears at first. He's thin and pale, but there's muscle along his narrow bones from years of traveling. Years of running. Dark curls of hair dust his chest and trail down from his belly button to surround the cock Arthur tasted yesterday.

He has more scars than the ones on his arms. Three white streaks cross his chest diagonally from collarbone to sternum. Puckered patches beneath his ribs. A whole stretch of tiny discolorations wrapping around his left thigh, quickly covered as Shae moves deeper into the water.

"Did you actually want a bath, or did you just want to stare at me?" Shae asks. There's an expression on his face that Arthur can't quite read.

"I just wanted to stare at you," Arthur answers immediately. "What is it?"

Shae wades closer, a scowl briefly deepening between his brows. For a moment, Arthur thinks he might not answer. But when he's close enough, he says, "The scar on your back."

Arthur goes still.

Funny. He was so concerned about Shae's scars that he forgot about his own.

One year ago, Ronan's blade slipped through his skin and muscle. Precisely angled not to kill him, but the poison swept straight through his bloodstream. Arthur's not exactly sure what it looks like now. It's inconvenient to check. The healers said there was barely a pink line to the left of his spine, but that was a year ago. He assumes it's healed more now, and it doesn't hurt or itch. Sometimes he forgets that his body carries a permanent reminder of his carelessness.

Shae must see something in his expression, because he murmurs, "Sorry."

"It's fine," Arthur says, reaching out his hand. "It doesn't hurt. Come here."

Shae joins Arthur in the middle of the river. He does as Arthur had, ducking down to get his head wet and burying his hands in his hair, but straightens back up with a curse almost immediately.

"What's wrong?" Arthur asks, wading closer.

Shae waves his left hand, the scabbed-over cut still visible down the palm. "There's a reason I usually stab myself in the arm instead. Ow."

He probably wouldn't appreciate the pang of guilt Arthur feels—though Arthur *is* grateful not to have been ripped apart by vaidkos in the middle of the road. He takes Shae's hand and kisses his fingertips. Savors the shiver that runs through Shae's body at the touch. He's never met anyone so responsive to the simplest things before.

"Want me to get your hair instead?"

He expects refusal or hesitation. Anything but Shae's immediate, "All right. Thanks."

Now Arthur's the one overwhelmed by the simple act of trust as he puts his hand on Shae's neck, and Shae bends over in the water. His hair flows around Arthur's hands, tangling between his fingers. His spine curves above the water, every vertebra visible. There aren't as many scars on his back. Shae claims he's spent ten years running from his fears, but his body tells a different story. The story of a man who faces danger head-on and bears the scars to prove it.

Arthur scrubs over Shae's scalp as best he can before feeling Shae move. He lets Shae back up in a splash. Water runs down from his drenched hair, sliding and sparkling over his jaw, his throat, his arms. His heaving chest. His lips part to gasp for air. Arthur's cock hardens in response.

"Let me get your back too," he suggests selfishly.

Shae shoves his drenched hair back from his face and wipes the water from his eyes. "You don't have to make excuses to touch me," he says, turning around. "Unless you're really excited about hygiene."

Arthur laughs. "You got me. I'm a clean freak."

Shae isn't tiny, but he feels and looks like it under Arthur's larger hands. He shivers with the first touch, leaning into the pressure as Arthur rubs the tense muscles of his shoulders. It's not much of a scrub-down. They don't have towels or soap. Just Arthur's callused hands scraping against Shae's skin, more a massage than anything else. The dirt washing away into the river is incidental. Even in the chill of the water, he feels Shae warming up beneath his touch.

"You said ages ago you could feel my aura," Arthur says eventually. "Can you feel it right now?"

"Yes," Shae breathes. His head tips back in pleasure, and his wet hair falls over Arthur's hands.

"What does it feel like? Heat?"

Shae turns around in his arms, a hungry light in his eyes. He touches Arthur's waist. His stomach. Places one hand at Arthur's neck, thumb stroking over his pulse point. They press together, and under the water, Arthur feels Shae's hot, hard cock slide up against his own.

"It's warm," Shae says quietly. "But it's more than that. If you could taste sunlight, it would taste like you. I haven't felt the heat of summer in so long, I've forgotten what it felt like. I've spent so long just trying to be *less cold*. Actually being warm was a pathetic fantasy."

"Shae," Arthur starts, heart pounding, but thin fingers cover his lips.

"When I'm near you," Shae whispers, "I feel alive."

The water runs around and between them, and living heat runs through Arthur's veins, pulling him to Shae. He covers Shae's mouth and swallows down every breath, every whimper he can get. Shae kisses back like a starving man, and Arthur wonders how he ever thought the necromancer was cold at heart.

He reaches between them and wraps his hand around both their cocks. Stroking them together is like liquid fire beneath Arthur's skin. The slight friction through the water, the way Shae rocks against him, up into his hand.

Shae moans into his mouth. Bracing his left wrist on Arthur's shoulder, he drops his right hand down to join Arthur's. Their fingers twine together around their cocks, and with a few rough strokes, Shae breaks from their kiss. His forehead presses to Arthur's chest, and he shudders through his orgasm.

Arthur quickly follows him, his lungs and veins filled entirely with Shae.

SHAE

The last few days to Lanwatch pass in a blur of heat and tender touches. They don't go further than using each other's hands again, and while Shae would like to do more, he's overwhelmed enough with what he has.

In some ways, the paladin's presence feels the same as ever. Warm, reassuring, companionable. Funny. But knowing his desire is returned, knowing that Arthur's smile and the way he occasionally touches Shae's arm aren't just because he's doing a job? Whenever he looks at Arthur and finds Arthur looking at him too, Shae can't help smiling like a lovestruck fool.

"You're cheerful today," Arthur says, grinning right back. "Any good news to share?"

Shae tries to compose his expression, and fails spectacularly. "Oh, you know. It's just such lovely weather."

Arthur reaches out and takes his hand, lacing their fingers together. He doesn't flinch when he touches silver, and Shae's palm throbs with the contact. "You're right," he murmurs, pulling Shae's hand up. "The weather's gorgeous."

Shae nearly combusts, all his blood rushing to his flushed face and his very interested cock, as Arthur kisses his knuckles.

They round the next corner together and come face to face with a bristling array of swords.

Shae nearly topples as Arthur shoves him back, and he can't see much besides Arthur's broad back. His heart flies into his throat, and he grabs for his knife.

A musical female voice rings out, "Halt there, travelers!"

The tension visibly eases from Arthur's shoulders, and his hand leaves his sword hilt. "I didn't know Riverswords were turning to robbery these days. Times must be hard."

"Weapons down, darlings," the same woman says. "Back off and keep watch."

Shae steps around Arthur's bulk. Seven men and women in well-worn leathers are sheathing their swords. Here and there is a flash of Riverswords blue—a scarf, an armband, a hat. One woman crosses her arms at the front of the pack, and the others step back to do her bidding, watching the road and the trees surrounding them.

"Apologies," the woman says, though she doesn't sound very sorry. She's nearly as tall as Arthur, and though she's far leaner, her bare arms are carved with muscle. Her black hair hangs in waves to her chiseled jaw, a wide streak to the left of her face colored brilliant Riverswords blue. "My little dears are jumpy right now. I'm Georgia Oakven. And you are?"

Shae's steadying heart rate picks up again at the name. The first name sounds Charaini enough, but the last name? Either the woman herself or her bloodline are from Lyrisenia. Probably not uncommon, this close to the border, but Shae feels an unfamiliar pang of kinship.

Arthur reaches his hand out. "Arthur Davorin, of the Radiant Order, and this is—"

"Shaesarenna Nightven," Shae says, before Arthur can speak for him. "Call me Shae. Why are your people jumpy?"

Georgia ignores Arthur's hand until he drops it, turning her attention to Shae instead. She looks Shae up and down with palpable interest in his rings. Not the usual disgust. "A necromancer and a paladin, huh." She gestures to Arthur as she answers Shae. "We're hunting vaidkos like we were hired to, no thanks to their little order stampeding through the forest."

"There are other paladins around?" Shae asks. He glances at Arthur, who looks unsurprised, even though the nearest Varan church should be halfway across Charain. "Why are they here?"

"You aren't with them? They're hunting some petty thief. Near turned over every rock in Lanwatch looking for him before they pranced off."

"Do you know who they're looking for?" Arthur asks, frowning. There's a tension in his voice Shae can't quite place.

Georgia shrugs. "No clue. My darlings and I have our hands full hunting vaidkos." She nods at Shae. "Are you looking for work, necromancer? We could use some of your blood witchery if you're available."

A skinny, silver-haired man steps up to Georgia's shoulder. He glares daggers at Shae. "Captain, I'm not sure about—"

"Tell me later, dear," she says without turning around. "Are you looking for work?"

Shae stares. He's worked with Riverswords in the past, and not all of them stole his boots or left him asleep and alone in the middle of the forest. Most of them took his coin and accompanied him from one town to the next and then left, as quick as they could. He hires them, not the other way around. Mercenaries never seek him out for his expertise.

That's the purview of desperate people haunted by spirits that won't let go. People he can help. And people he can't—the grieving parents wanting their children back. Widows and widowers wanting their spouses. Heartsick children who want their parents, or somebody, anybody.

"I'm not available," he says. "But if there's a vaidkos outbreak around here, it may be related to something we've been running across."

She raises an eyebrow, somehow making the gesture look effortless. "Oh?"

"They're eating souls," Shae says. "So, stake out any local graveyards and abandoned churches. They're teleporting in, but I don't know if they can teleport out. Either way, they'll be tough to track, so you'll have better luck going to their feeding grounds."

Arthur adds, "We also ran across a possessed corpse a day south of here. Be on your guard."

"Moon Mother's tits," Georgia swears. Then her scowl breaks into a grin, fierce and bright. "Hey Reed, think we can wrangle hazard pay out of the Lanwatch council if we find a demon too?"

The silver-haired man replies, "They're cheapskates, but give me an hour with them."

"Good man." She runs her hand through her hair, messing it up even more. "Well, Shae, Arthur, thanks for the information. Guess we're off to a graveyard next."

"Light guide you," Arthur says, and they move on.

Shae follows Arthur and Duchess past the mercenaries. Most of them clearly aren't as recklessly accepting as their captain, and he catches a few warding gestures and averted eyes. A chill sinks through his stomach, despite the heat of Arthur's presence beside him.

These past couple of weeks with Arthur, he's barely interacted with other people. When they stop in towns and villages, Arthur handles the social aspects. Shae hadn't realized what a relief it was until the weight of distrust and suspicion settled over his shoulders again.

"You all right?" Arthur says quietly, when they're well out of the Riverswords' earshot.

I'm never all right, Shae wants to say. Instead he answers shortly, "I'm fine."

He's not sure if he's grateful or resentful that Arthur doesn't press further.

It's stupid to be upset about the way people look at him. He should be used to it by now. Besides, he only has to deal with it for a little longer. He just needs to get through the final leg of this journey, and everything will be over. Everything will be better.

The road evens out, better maintained the closer they get to Lanwatch. Crossroads with weather-worn signs leading to other outposts become more frequent, and they even start to come across other travelers. All of them armed, merchants and hunters alike, and none of them alone. Clearly the locals are well aware of the vaidkos problem.

Arthur stops Duchess on the side of the road every time a cart approaches, waiting for it to pass. Shae thinks he's just being polite the first few times, until he notices how intently Arthur is examining each passing traveler.

"What are you looking for?" he asks as a cart of merchants rumbles past them. The cart turns at the crossroads, heading west, its occupants staring at Arthur and Shae alike.

Arthur's perfectly stubbled face holds a more distant expression than Shae is used to. "I'm seeing if I recognize anyone. Oakven said there were order members in the area."

"They should stand out like a sore thumb though, wouldn't they?" Shae gestures to Arthur's tunic, bright white and emblazoned with the golden sun. Even travel-stained and mended, the garment is recognizable. "You lot aren't exactly subtle."

Arthur laughs at that. The sound is a welcome brightness. "You're right about that." He tugs Duchess away from inspecting the foliage at the edge of the road and starts moving again.

"Do you guys usually patrol so far north?" Shae asks. "I don't think any paladin order had a presence here last time I passed through."

"We don't," Arthur says. "I think this is the same group that rode through Hannick. The shopkeeper there told me they were riding through fast."

Shae frowns, suddenly unsettled. "I don't think you told me about that." The words come out sulkier than he wanted them to.

After feeling so in-tune with Arthur, it's strange to remember the man still has his own life and priorities outside Shae. It shouldn't be strange, though. Arthur's been in the Radiant Order for seven years now, while he's been Shae's bodyguard for a couple of weeks. Whatever relationship they have together now, Shae doesn't come first.

"I thought I had," Arthur says with a shrug. Then he grins at Shae, a wicked gleam in his green eyes. "Maybe I was distracted by something."

That smile is deadly to Shae's composure. Against his will, his lips twitch in an answering grin. "I have no idea what you're talking about."

"Then I'll have to show you."

Arthur leans down for a kiss. His hand slides to Shae's waist, holding him steady as he steals Shae's breath. Shae closes his eyes, trying to burn his worries away in the heat. The sensation of stubble scratching his cheek, another man's pulse quickening under his fingers.

It even almost works.

ARTHUR

Beyond Lanwatch's sharp-slanting wooden roofs, the occasional blue light of the Northern Barrier flickers in the sky. On paper, the town isn't much smaller than Andell, but half the population lives in smaller settlements in the surrounding woods or along the river. The actual center of town feels like a hollow shell, with too few people in too many buildings. There are plenty of taverns, but only one working inn.

"Why don't you wait out here while I rent us a room?" Arthur asks, hitching Duchess outside.

He means it as a favor—it's no secret how little Shae likes any other person they've encountered—but Shae's face goes cold at the suggestion. "That's a good idea," he says, even though his stiff posture indicates the opposite. "Go ahead."

"You don't have to," Arthur says, frowning. "I just thought you'd prefer it."

"No, you're right." Shae twists one of his rings. "Better I stay out here. You go on."

"I'll be right inside if you need anything." Arthur wants to lean in for a kiss goodbye—he wants any excuse to kiss Shae, now that he knows he can—but Shae doesn't seem amenable to that at all right now. There are enough random passersby around, and Arthur doesn't know how Shae feels about public displays of affection. They haven't talked about that at all.

They haven't talked about a lot of things, really.

Unease settles into Arthur's stomach as he heads into the inn, though he tries to shake it off. Maybe Shae's just annoyed to be around other people again. He's been prickly on and off since they ran across the Riverswords on the road.

Jessop the innkeeper doesn't have any more information than Georgia Oakven about the paladins nearby. Just confirmation that they tore up the town searching for someone, then headed west. As he negotiates for a room and meal, Arthur wonders if he should ride west to meet them. It's selfish—he has his duty to Shae—but he misses the sense of belonging and companionship. The certainty of following orders and knowing that all he does is Vara's will.

"Light guide you," he says to Jessop as he leaves.

☽○☾

THEIR ROOM FOR the night has a single bed, covered in an abominably bright green and yellow quilt. That and the orange curtains nearly disguise the fact that the furniture is all dull and chipped, the walls more yellow than white.

Shae goes to the window and pulls the curtains open. He leans with his hands on the windowsill, and the late afternoon sun streams in around the narrow lines of his body. "Lanwatch looks the same as it used to. I thought it would seem smaller or something."

Arthur sets his sword on the table and their packs on the floor, then sits on the edge of the bed and starts taking off his boots. "You've been here before?"

"On my way south, after—yes." Shae plays with the edge of the curtain. "It was the biggest city I'd ever seen."

Arthur laughs. Stretches his toes out, rolls his sore ankles. "All of Lanwatch could fit in the district I grew up in." He's exaggerating, but not by much.

"There aren't many large settlements left in Lyrisenia. My—my family lived ten miles outside a village of about fifty people, and we only visited a few times a year." Shae turns around and leans back against the windowsill. Backlit, Arthur has to squint to see his face. "Sorry. I don't know why I'm talking about this."

There's a pang in Arthur's chest. "There doesn't need to be a reason. I don't mind."

"I mind." Shae pushes away from the window and crosses the room to check the door latch. He moves to the table and starts unlacing his boots. He keeps moving, like a prowling wolf. Or maybe he's the deer, always on the run, looking over his shoulder. "Last time I was here, nobody looked twice at me. I didn't have the rings and charms yet. I didn't know I'd need them. I didn't feel the cold yet."

The words are rough, like they're dragging themselves from his unwilling throat.

"You won't have to deal with that anymore soon, right?" Arthur says. "Once you banish the demon, you'll be able to take the rings off. Nobody will know what you were."

Shae glances towards the window, and the sunlight gilds his expressionless face. "Right. Everything will be fine, afterwards." He whips around to stare at Arthur. There's no sunlight in his gaze, just burning cold. "And I won't have to leech off people for warmth anymore."

There's a question there, or an accusation, prickling under Arthur's skin. "I'll admit, that part of it hasn't been bad for me."

It must be the right thing to say. A smile curves Shae's lips, and he stalks forward barefoot. "Is that so?" He comes to a halt at the edge of the bed and settles himself in Arthur's lap, straddling his thighs. He breathes against Arthur's lips, "I'm cold right now. Would you mind warming me up?"

Arthur answers with a kiss, tasting the chill of Shae's mouth. Shae opens up to him easily and lets him explore. The touch warms Arthur too, pulling blood close to the skin with hums of pleasure. Every time Shae moves, their cocks rub through their clothing. The friction and pressure are so sweet that given time, Arthur could come from this alone.

Shae seems to have more ambitious plans than that. He breaks away, panting slightly. "Will you fuck me?"

Arthur groans and grabs Shae's ass. Squeezes the firm flesh and tugs him in closer, harder. "Yes. Absolutely, yes."

Shae kisses him again, rough and ravenous, until Arthur bites his lip and says, "Take your clothes off for me." He gives Shae's ass one more squeeze before letting him go.

While Shae strips, Arthur looks through his pack for the jar of denseed oil—though he keeps glancing over his shoulder to take in the show. He doesn't think he'll ever get tired of watching Shae's layers fall away, baring all that pale, scarred skin for Arthur, and Arthur alone. He'll definitely never get tired of the hungry expression in Shae's eyes. The way that silver gaze digs under his own skin, seeking for the very core of him.

Shae's down to his unlaced trousers when Arthur rejoins him. He tosses the oil on the bed and slides his hands around Shae's waist. His fingers dip beneath his waistband, digging into the curves of his ass, as he drags Shae towards him. Shae's breath hitches, and he tugs at Arthur's tunic. "Fair's fair."

"Are you sure?" Arthur grins. "People usually think the uniform is dashing."

"It'll look more dashing on the floor."

"I'll trust your judgment," Arthur says, and reluctantly lets go of Shae's ass to strip his clothes off. It's worth it for the way Shae looks at him, like a feast he's ready to devour. Desire flares between them like an all-consuming fire.

Shae finally takes his trousers off, nearly tripping as they catch around his ankle. As soon as he straightens, Arthur crowds into him, touching his neck, his waist, his hip. Shae kisses his neck, with a hint of teeth that takes Arthur's breath away. They stagger to the bed still entwined and fall onto it together.

The next few moments are a blur of bare skin and clawing hands, limbs sliding against limbs, mouths barely reaching mouths in their desperation to kiss. Arthur has to sit back and dig the heel of his hand into the base of his cock, breathing through the pleasure, to keep from orgasming too soon.

He opens his eyes and sees Shae sprawled out on the gaudy green and yellow quilt, his skin starkly pale and his hair fanning soft around his face. His eyes are the same bright silver as the rings in his ears. His legs spread on either side of Arthur, hiding nothing.

Arthur reaches for the oil, mouth dry with want. "Tell me if any of this hurts, all right?"

A smirk ghosts on Shae's lips. "You don't have to go easy on me, paladin."

"What if I want to?" Arthur leans down and kisses Shae's stomach. Feels the soft flesh jump under his lips. "You're very handsome, and I like you a lot. I want you to feel good."

"It'll feel good," Shae says, wrapping his ankle behind Arthur's hip, "if you get around to fucking me before the sun sets."

Arthur swears and kisses the inside of Shae's knee on his way back up. "You're in a rush today, huh?"

Shae just licks his lower lip.

Arthur dips his fingers into the denseed oil and sets the jar on the bedside table. He braces himself on one arm and focuses entirely on Shae's face as his hand falls between the man's thighs. Shae's eyes flutter close as Arthur palms his cock. Rolls his balls and hears the sweetest, hottest whine from that thin throat. He slides his fingers down Shae's taint and rubs the rim of his hole, and Shae's lips part, panting for breath.

"I think we have another two hours until sunset," Arthur says contemplatively. "Plenty of time."

Shae groans and covers his face with his arm. "I will actually murder you."

Then his hands fly to claw at the quilt as Arthur's forefinger pushes into his ass. Arthur can't keep pretending to go slow; the feeling of Shae around his finger is instantly addictive. Shae's so hot and responsive to every slight movement, his body clinging to Arthur's fingers. Arthur pushes a second finger in, and there's a tension that recedes as he keeps moving. Quicker pumps than Arthur intended, maybe still too slow for Shae. He presses up, adjusting his angle until—

Arching off the mattress, Shae gasps, "Gods, there. Right there."

Arthur massages into the same spot, dizzy with how hot Shae is writhing beneath him, until he can't take the waiting anymore. He withdraws his fingers and spills out a palmful of oil to slick up his cock. The touch of his own hand is nothing, but the thought of sheathing himself inside Shae's waiting body nearly sends him over the edge again. Deep breaths help, and he hikes Shae's legs up around his hips.

They join together slowly. Arthur's too overwhelmed to crack more jokes, and Shae stops demanding that Arthur go faster. Every inch of Arthur's cock slides into Shae's body with agonizingly sweet pressure and heat. The oil is the only thing between them. He lowers himself to his elbow as he sinks to the hilt, and Shae's arms wind shakily around his shoulders, then tighten. Holding him down.

Arthur meant to warn Shae before he moved, but he's breathless with pleasure and his body has other ideas. His hips jerk, drawing a sweet groan from Shae, and another when he thrusts back in. As he moves, Shae only holds him tighter, buries his hands in Arthur's hair, and drags him into a messy kiss.

Their lips slide together. Sometimes he kisses Shae's mouth, sometimes his jaw, sometimes his ear. "Touch yourself while I fuck you," he murmurs, then breaks off in a groan as Shae tightens around him. "I want you to come on my cock."

Shae's only answer is a whimper, but one of his hands untangles from his hair and drops between them.

They find a rough, artless rhythm, and eventually, Shae is the first to come. He bites into Arthur's shoulder with a strangled yell, and his body clenches down in spasms around Arthur. He falls back, panting and flushed and dazed, and it's the sight of him more than the sensation that finally sends Arthur over the edge as well. His orgasm rolls through him like a thunder-cloud, and he shudders his release into Shae's body.

Arthur hangs there, panting for breath, until Shae extricates his remaining hand from his hair. Now free, though he's not sure he wants to be, he pecks a gentle kiss on Shae before sitting back on his heels and pulling out. A drop of come is visible on Shae's rim, and the sight satisfies some primal, possessive urge inside Arthur.

He collapses next to Shae and presses his forehead against the man's narrow shoulder. "Still want to murder me?"

Shae laughs breathlessly. "You're safe for tonight, brave paladin." He turns onto his side, facing the window. Arthur brushes the hair from his neck to press a single kiss there, then settles naturally behind him. His spent cock rests against Shae's ass, and Shae's ribs rise and fall against his.

He should be washing up, getting dressed. Going around town and asking about vaidkos and paladins and petty thieves. But his body's filled with languid satiation, and he'd rather stay another few moments with Shae in his arms.

SHAE

Shae picks at his breakfast and ignores the way Jessop the innkeeper avoids eye contact. Right now, he doesn't care if the man thinks he's about to summon corpses at the breakfast table; he just wants his ham and toast, and an entire pot of shaflower tea to wake him up. The inn's front room is cozy, with more bright curtains and blue-painted tabletops. Shae and a pair of merchants by the window are the only guests at the moment. They either don't notice Shae or don't care.

A slight chill creeps through his bones even as the warm food settles in his stomach. Arthur needed to check on Duchess, and Shae had said he should get the lay of the town while he was out. Usually Shae would insist on going with him, but he trusts Arthur to come back before he gets too cold. At least, he wants to trust him.

And Shae could use twenty minutes or so to breathe on his own. Savor the soreness lingering deep within his body. It's hard to think about anything when Arthur's right next to him, impossibly bright and attractive and distracting.

Now that Shae's alone, he's able to admit maybe sex isn't the solution to everything. He's glad they fucked—truly, viscerally glad—but his desperation and urgency were driven by anxiety as much as desire. He doesn't like being near people who hate him. He doesn't like thinking that other paladins might be around with a claim on Arthur's time and attention.

At least instead of just being anxious, now he's well-fucked and anxious.

He's only halfway through his first mug of tea when a familiar warm aura brushes his awareness. Shae swallows his tea and glances over as the front door swings open, and a tall stranger with Vara's sun on his chest walks in.

Shae reels, stunned.

The paladin is stouter than Arthur, paler and clean-shaven. His light brown hair is pulled back in a knot behind his head, and a long sky-blue cloak billows behind him. He calls out as he enters, "Jessop, my good man! A pint of ale, as fast as you can pour it!"

"Sir Bernard!" The innkeeper emerges from the kitchen, wiping his hands on his apron. His cheer sounds strained. "I thought you lot were gone west."

"I thought so too, but well—confidential details. I'm afraid I can't say more."

Their voices drop to a low enough volume that Shae can't eavesdrop without effort. He turns back to his tea, unsure whether he's amused or disgusted. Sir Bernard's arrogance wafts through the room like a sour perfume. Shae decides to finish eating quickly and return to their rented room. Or should he try to find Arthur in town? Head him off? He stares into the pink-gold shaflower tea, mind racing. Every selfish instinct tells him to keep Arthur away from this man.

The familiar but unfamiliar aura intensifies. Shae's head whips up as Sir Bernard strides towards him, cloak billowing unnecessarily.

"Necromancer," he says, far more loudly than necessary. Shae is too aware of the way the merchants at the window table drop their utensils to listen in. "I'm from the Radiant Order, and I need to ask you a few questions."

Shae clenches his jaw. On the one hand, his entire body craves the warmth emanating from the paladin's spirit. On the other hand, his ten years' experience with self-important men like this tells him to run out of the room or draw his knife. Neither instinct is particularly helpful.

He finishes his mug of tea. "Unfortunately, I don't have any answers."

Bernard sets his hand on the table in front of Shae. Not slamming it, but hard enough to jolt the empty mug. "My friend Jessop says you came into town yesterday. What are you doing in Lanwatch?"

"Currently?" Shae gestures at his plate. "Eating toast."

Bernard's smile isn't friendly at all. "You think you're funny, don't you?"

Shae bites back another snarky reply with all the willpower he has left. Where the fuck is Arthur? Should he mention Arthur to this guy? But Bernard doesn't seem like the sort of guy who actually wants answers, or who'll believe anything Shae says. He needs to figure out what Bernard *does* want—or get out of here before he gets into a fight.

"My apologies," Shae says, though it kills him to say it. "What are your important questions about?"

Bernard's frown doesn't soften at all. "You'll need to come with me. We'll talk with my commander."

Absolutely not. Shae's palm itches for the hilt of his knife. "My apologies," Shae repeats, like the words are a ritual spell. "I'm waiting for my friend. He's actually in your Radiant Order too, you might know him."

"Sure, sure." Bernard finally grins. He touches a chain at his throat, and a familiar warmth washes over Shae's frayed nerves. "Why don't you tell me *exactly* who your friend is?"

Truth spell. The bastard used a truth spell on him.

Shae shoves to his feet, nearly knocking over his chair as he backs up. "You have no jurisdiction over me," he snaps, which is the utter truth. "I'm going upstairs."

He glances around, making eye contact with Jessop and the two merchants in turn. All of them are watching, but none of them speak up to interfere. Not even Jessop, who knows Shae came in yesterday with a paladin of the Radiant Order.

"Tell me," Bernard says, stepping into Shae's path. "You dark mages always like to stick together. Are you with the heretic?"

Every nerve in Shae's body screams to run. He hasn't decided whether to answer or deflect, hasn't decided which one is the safest route, when a familiar, welcome voice calls out across the front room.

"Bernard? I saw your horse outside, I can't believe—what's going on here?" Arthur stands in the doorway, looking between the two of them. Gratitude rushes through Shae, as warm as the touch of Arthur's aura.

Bernard breaks into a smile. "Arthur! Radiance, it's good to see you." He gestures to Shae. "I was just bringing this necromancer in for questioning."

Arthur steps forward, his beautiful brow furrowed. "Shae's with me," he says, putting his hand on Shae's shoulder. Shae can't resist leaning into the touch. "What in Vara's name are you questioning him about?"

"He was being a sanctimonious asshole," Shae says, pulling away from Arthur's touch. He loves it, he craves it, but his skin prickles with annoyance at the entire situation. He wants Arthur to swoop in and save him—but he hates that he needs him to. "And Sir Bernard here can assure you I'm speaking the truth."

"Listen here, necromancer—" Bernard starts, but Arthur interrupts.

"You used a truth spell on him?" His frown deepens. "Take it off."

Arthur's annoyance is a little rich, Shae thinks as he sits back down, considering that Arthur also once used a truth spell on him without warning. *Maybe the rules are different for necromancers you've fucked.* He pours himself another mug of tea from the pot, the action helping keep his mind steady and stopping him from spouting out more dangerous truths.

Bernard scowls for a moment, then breaks into a

laugh. He waves his hand, and the cage of light lifts from Shae's mind. Tension vanishes from Shae's neck.

"Sorry, sorry, just a misunderstanding. I had no idea he was a friend of yours." Bernard looks around at the innkeeper and the unrepentantly staring merchants. "Sorry for the disturbance, everyone, nothing to see here. Jessop! Can you bring out some more food with that ale?"

Like another spell's been broken, everyone starts moving again. Jessop vanishes back into the kitchen, and the merchants drop coin on their table before leaving the inn. Arthur sits down to Shae's left, and Bernard—to Shae's immediate annoyance—sits across from Arthur, to Shae's right.

Shae doesn't miss that Bernard has apologized to everyone in the room except him.

"How have you been, Bernard?" Arthur asks. "What's the order doing this far north? Who's leading?" His hand drops under the table to briefly squeeze Shae's thigh, in a gesture that Shae doesn't understand. Is he trying to comfort him? Warn him? Tell him to stay quiet while he gets information out of Bernard?

Shae wants more than anything to run out the door, find Duchess and bury his face in her mane. Run out to the river and scream underwater. But something in him is afraid to leave Arthur alone with Bernard. Not that he thinks Bernard will hurt Arthur—and that's the problem.

The innkeeper brings out the food and ale Bernard requested, then returns to the kitchen.

Bernard swigs from the ale. "Captain Tanner's in command," he says. "She'll be happy to see you.

Keeps complaining that the rest of us aren't making up the slack."

"She always complains about me too." A grin creeps into Arthur's voice.

Shae pours more tea. He feels invisible, and Arthur's immediate camaraderie with this asshole does nothing to ease his nerves.

"No way, you were always her favorite." Bernard sets his ale down and leans in. Lowers his voice. "As for what we're doing here, well. Vara himself must have guided you here too."

For some reason, Arthur stiffens at his side. Shae's stomach twists in an inexplicable sense of dread.

Arthur asks, "Is it him?"

"Yeah," Bernard answers. "We're closing in on Ronan Vizia."

ARTHUR

The room seems to sink and rise unevenly around Arthur. He feels sick, the same way he felt the day his world turned upside down, like he still has Ronan's knife lodged cold beneath his ribs. Like he's still standing on the white marble floor of the Bright Cathedral, facing the High Commander and Archpriest on his own. Praying for forgiveness, ready for damnation. Ready for anything except this unbearable year of limbo.

He remembers Ronan's smile. The taste of his skin, now ashes in Arthur's mouth.

"Radiance," he swears, or prays. He isn't sure if there's a difference right now. He rubs his hand over his face. "I can't believe it's taken so long to find him."

"We wouldn't have found him at all, except he hit another church last month. Not one of ours, he stole a relic of Mother Sephine's this time. He's been giving us a hell of a chase." Bernard downs half his ale and wipes his mouth, then leans back in again. "I can't say much, but we're only camped an hour out of town. You should meet with Captain Tanner. She can fill you in on the rest, and maybe if she's talking to you, she'll leave off yelling at the rest of us for a few minutes."

Arthur wants to say yes, but he stops himself. Glances to Shae, who sits pale and tense beside him. "I can't," he says, grimacing. "I haven't finished my penance yet, and I'm on a job right now."

I can't abandon Shae, he doesn't add, because he knows Bernard won't understand. For all his faults, Bernard has always put the Radiant Order above everything. He expects nothing less from Arthur.

"Your penance forbids you from walking into a church, not from walking into a camp," Bernard says. "Come on, how many weeks do you even have left?"

"Just under a month," Arthur answers. "But it doesn't matter. I'm committed to this job for the next week. If you leave word here, maybe we can meet up when I'm free?"

Bernard shakes his head and finishes his mug. "If we haven't caught Vizia by then, Captain will have all our pendants as well as our heads. Vara willing, we'll be long gone."

Shae touches his arm. Arthur is hyper-aware of the way his skin tingles under Shae's hand, and the way Bernard watches intently. The man acts like a buffoon sometimes, but he notices more than you'd expect.

"Can we talk alone?" Shae asks.

They move towards the window while Bernard calls

out for another ale. The bright morning sun doesn't seem to touch Shae's face at all, like his skin is still shaded with clouds and moonlight.

"What is it?" Arthur asks quietly.

Shae twists one of his rings. Arthur can't help reaching out and covering Shae's hands in his, holding him still. Shae freezes for a moment, then holds onto him. "I know this is important to you," he says hesitantly. "Will seeing this Captain Tanner help at all?"

Arthur's grip tightens involuntarily. He forces himself to let go, aware of Bernard watching across the room. "I thought I was fine waiting until my year was up," he says eventually. "But knowing they're all right there—knowing they have more information about Ronan—he ruined my life, Shae. I want to know what he really did it for."

Shae gives a shaky sigh. "This Bernard is an asshole, and if the rest of them are like that, I'm not looking forward to it. But we can spare half a day if it means that much to you."

"You caught Bernard on a bad day. He's—driven." Arthur had panicked when he ran in and saw Shae and Bernard facing off, but Bernard had backed down when he realized there was a problem. Arthur doesn't blame Shae for not liking him, though.

"Sure." Shae twists his ring again, and this time Arthur resists the urge to hold him still. "We can spare half a day. No more."

A wave of gratitude rushes through Arthur. He grins down at Shae. "You're the best. Thank you."

"Sure," Shae says again, and heads for the stairs without another word.

$$)O($$

THEY SET OUT from Lanwatch an hour later, most of which was spent buying a horse for Shae. Arthur helps him pick the calmest-seeming horse available at the stable—a sturdy, dark gelding with long ears and a star between his eyes. The stablemaster tells them his name is Sparrow, and throws in the tack at a discount. The gelding is small enough that Shae manages to mount from the ground, with some coaching from Arthur and trial and error.

The ride out is mostly quiet. Bernard and Shae don't seem inclined to talk to each other, leaving Arthur awkwardly in the middle of their silent feud. Arthur spends most of the ride watching Shae to make sure he's adjusting to the new horse, and he spends the rest of the time thinking about Ronan.

He hasn't thought about Ronan much over the past week or so. He's been so caught up in Shae, he's forgotten to ruminate on his hurts. The betrayal gnaws at him again now, just as fresh as the day Ronan stabbed him.

Guilt gnaws at him too. What kind of penance is this, if he stops reflecting on his mistakes?

A week before his life was ruined, they lay in bed as the sun rose. Ronan was as tall as Arthur, nearly as broad, and they barely fit in Arthur's bed. Ronan had said, "Did you know it's my birthday tomorrow?"

He had a way of starting a conversation that made people excited to hear the rest of it. A con artist's charisma.

"I know now." Arthur vividly remembers rolling over in bed, rumpled cotton sheets tangled around his legs. Kissing the sleep from Ronan's lips. "What do you want? Dinner? Drinks? Sex? A new belt? Sex?"

Ronan laughed and kissed him breathless. Pulled back and said, eyes sparkling, "I've actually always wanted to see the Dawn's Tomb."

The most heavily guarded chamber in the Bright Cathedral, where the Radiant Crown was kept.

The request seemed weird at the time. It was the only ingenuine thing Arthur ever sensed about Ronan. His faith always felt shallow, insincere, more concerned with buildings and rites and objects of worship than with Vara's Radiance itself. All of the logistics and tools, none of the emotion. Arthur thought sometimes that Ronan was pretending to be more faithful than he was.

He thought, because he was a fool, that Ronan was pretending because he loved him.

The next day—looking back now, Arthur doesn't even know if that day was really Ronan's birthday—he showed Ronan the Dawn's Tomb. Just the door outside, they couldn't go in, but that was bad enough. They kissed under the statue of the Radiant, and one week later, Ronan used that knowledge of the layout to break in and steal the Crown of Vara.

Leaving Arthur bleeding out and utterly lost.

He's found more pieces of himself than he expected over the past year. Most of them over the past few weeks with Shae. But maybe it's a mistake to think he can fully move on with this question of *why* hanging over his head. He can't commit himself fully to Shae *or* Vara when part of him is still caught up in Ronan.

The order is camped in a hollow clearing, just off the road. A freshly cleared trail leads from the road to the camp. Arthur counts enough tents for two dozen, including squires, but only sees a handful of people around. A woman with dark brown skin and short hair takes one look at them riding in and ducks into the largest tent. Freya. They graduated in the same class five years ago.

Riding into camp should feel like coming home. Familiar white and gold banners everywhere, familiar armor, familiar faces. Even the layout is familiar—all the smaller tents in a grid surrounding the mess tent and the captain's tent. But as two squires come forward to tether their horses, Arthur feels out of place. He has an odd sense that everyone's looking at him, and not everyone is as happy to see him as Bernard.

Shae stumbles as he dismounts, and Arthur moves forward on instinct to steady him. But Shae recovers and steps away before they touch. His face is wooden.

"Captain's tent is this way," Bernard says unnecessarily. The tent is three times the size of any others.

Also unnecessary, because seconds later, Captain Edith Tanner emerges from her tent. Her height always takes Arthur by surprise—she barely comes up to his shoulders, but her presence fills the entire campsite. Her long golden hair is braided in a crown around her head, while her clothing and expression are ruthlessly utilitarian.

"Arthur Davorin," she calls out. "I hardly believed Freya's words. What brings you here?"

"Captain." Arthur bows his head. "I ran into Bernard in Lanwatch, and he said we should talk." He looks up, trying to read Tanner's expression. Should he have come? Was trusting Bernard a mistake? "If I may, it's good to see you, Captain."

Tanner looks him up and down, steel in her eyes. Her eyebrows rise when she sees Shae next to him. But when she turns back to Arthur, it's with a smile. "It's good to see you too, Arthur. Bernard's right, we should talk." She points at Shae. "But first, this is…?"

There's an awkward pause in which Shae doesn't introduce himself. He just glances to Arthur, who has to step up. "This is Shae Nightven. He hired me for a job, and he's a friend of mine."

It feels oddly like introducing Shae to his mother. Except his mother would probably be a more welcoming audience. This would be a hell of a lot easier if Shae tried at all to be friendly.

"Hi," Shae says, deadpan.

"A friend," Tanner repeats, equally deadpan. She turns back to Arthur. "Let's talk inside. Freya, can you lead Arthur's *friend* to the mess tent to wait? If that's all right, Arthur?"

"Shae?" Arthur doesn't want to explicitly ask if Shae will be all right alone. The man definitely wouldn't thank him for voicing the concern out loud.

Shae plays with an earring, at least outwardly unconcerned. All he says is, "Don't take too long," before following Freya.

Arthur stares after him, then follows Tanner into her tent. It's tall enough to stand comfortably, and with her rank, she gets an actual cot, not a bedroll like the rank and file. There's even a fold-out table covered in paper and a mug, with two chairs. Here, the wave of nostalgia finally knocks him truly off-balance. Arthur has stood at this flimsy fold-out table dozens of times, receiving assignments or giving reports.

As soon as the tent flap swings shut behind them, Tanner sinks onto one of the chairs with a sigh. She waves to the other chair. "It really is good to see you, Arthur. Even if you are riding up with a necromancer, of all things."

Arthur sits at her silent command, trying not to bristle at the dismissive tone in her voice. It's not her fault she doesn't know how amazing, selfless, brave, beautiful—well. Not her fault she doesn't know Shae at all. "He's a good man, sir."

She shakes her head. "I believe you," she says, though she sounds skeptical. "It just doesn't look great. Especially considering your, well. Your historical choices in companions."

He crosses his arms, no longer trying not to bristle. "Shae is nothing like Ronan. I swear on my pendant."

Tanner sounds a lot more tired than she sounded outside. "I didn't get the chance to talk to you after the hearing last year, and I regret that."

"There was a lot going on, Captain."

"I told Archpriest Neradt and the rest of the circle that I didn't agree with penance exile. I want you to know that." She grabs the mug on the table, then sets it back down.

Arthur shifts, trying to find a comfortable angle in the fold-out chair. "I appreciate that," he says. "It's been hard, but it hasn't all been bad. I've managed to do a lot of good over the past year."

Tanner waves her hand. "You were doing good in the order. We should have held a trial right then—the worst you'd have gotten was one month confinement, and then you'd be free and clear. Instead, we had to drag this on all year, and it's not looking good for the trial now."

Premonition swoops through Arthur's stomach, like a hawk diving for its prey. "What do you mean, sir?"

Tanner leans her elbows on the table, crumpling a few maps. "This information doesn't leave this tent," she says. The lines on her face look deeper than they used to. "This is an order matter, and the last thing we need is the crown meddling in order affairs. But we've learned Vizia has ties with Praia."

"Radiance," Arthur breathes.

"We could sure use some Radiance right now." She rubs the bridge of her nose. "I'll be honest, it's a mess. We're going to catch him soon, no doubt about it, and we're going to handle everything before filling the crown in, but the circle is panicking."

"I can imagine," Arthur says, even though he really can't. He never paid much attention to politics and strategy in the Radiant Order. He followed orders, and he served the faithful and the light of Vara. Tension between the secular government and Charain's myriad religious orders is beyond him. "You are close to getting him, right? Bernard said you were."

"We finally managed to get a tracking trace on him a week ago," she says, a hint of satisfaction in her smile. "He can keep running, but he can't hide, and he's not getting to Praia before we catch up."

"Good. That's good." Arthur shifts again on the uncomfortable chair. He still can't shake the premonition of danger. Tanner still hasn't answered his real question. "My penance is almost over. What do you mean about the trial not looking good?"

She sighs, and she looks kinder and more sympathetic than he's ever seen her. He's more used to her barking orders and scolding everyone in sight. "You've been one of my best paladins since the day you graduated, and I always thought someday you might replace me. But this whole situation is getting too political, and the Exalted Circle needs more scapegoats than just Vizia."

"You're saying they're going to sentence me more harshly than they would have otherwise." Arthur rubs his face, trying to get his thoughts in order. A month in confinement? Two months? Docked salary? None of those seem serious enough for the expression on Tanner's face.

She sighs again. "They might expel you from the order, Arthur."

Arthur freezes. There's a moment of blankness as the words echo through him. Until his heart thuds back into motion, quick and panicked.

He's spent all year without his brothers and sisters, without his chosen family and god-given purpose, driven only by the thought that when the year is over, he'll get them all back. The thought of losing everything hurts worse than anything Ronan ever did.

"He lied to me," he says eventually. "He stabbed me in the back, and he lied to me."

Tanner says quietly, "I know, boy. I know."

"Fuck. Sorry, I just." He leans against the table and covers his face in his hands. "Is that really likely?"

"That's what the circle had decided on, last I spoke with Neradt," she says. "Even though—wait. I've got an idea."

He drops his hands, feeling shaky.

Tanner continues, "They're worried about appearances. So, we need to have you make your grand return with an achievement they can't ignore, right?" A grin breaks across her face. "And since we're about a minute away from catching Ronan…"

Arthur would do just about anything to stay in the order. He leans in and hangs onto her every word.

SHAE

The Radiant Order's camp is one of the most disconcerting places Shae has ever been, and he's spent more time than most people in graveyards and mausoleums. Everyone around him has the same sun-bright aura as Arthur, to varying degrees. But unlike Arthur, they all stare at him with cold distrust.

The woman, Freya, leads him to a wide awning that covers a cookfire, supplies, and a few small tables. He sits at one of the tables as directed and tries not to make eye contact with anyone. It's easy. Everyone else is avoiding his gaze too.

He thought he was used to the glares and whispers everywhere he turns. Somehow it hurts more than it used to. Maybe that's his fault. He's avoided opening himself up to people for so long, until he met Arthur.

Of course, these are all Arthur's friends. Arthur fits in with them, and he doesn't realize they're being assholes to Shae because they aren't assholes to *him*. Because people treat people like Arthur differently than they treat people like Shae.

Maybe it's fair. Necromancy isn't pretty. But it still hurts.

Even though he knows it's a stupid, telling habit, Shae can't stop fiddling with his rings. There's more than enough ambient human warmth around to keep him from getting cold, but his stomach still twists with anxiety having Arthur out of sight. He doesn't like the way Captain Tanner looked at him. He doesn't like the way any of them looked at him.

Quiet voices catch his attention. Bernard and Freya talking just outside the mess tent. Shae strains to listen, but he can't make out any words. Every so often, they glance towards him.

After a moment, Freya claps Bernard on the shoulder and walks off. Bernard tosses his ridiculous cloak back and strides towards Shae. "Necromancer," he says, sitting down across from Shae. He's smiling, but it doesn't reach his eyes.

"Paladin," Shae says coolly.

But Bernard's next statement surprises him. "Sorry about earlier, by the way. Things have been a little high-tension with order business. You didn't hear this from me, but we have reason to think Vizia's involved with dark magic. So, when I saw a dark mage in the middle of Lanwatch..."

The apology knocks him off-kilter, even if it's followed by excuses. Bernard doesn't seem the type to justify himself to someone like Shae. "Arthur's told me a bit about him," Shae says. "But I don't work with other dark mages, or thieves."

"That's great." Bernard looks over his shoulder, then leans in. "You and Arthur seem pretty close, huh."

Shae's eyes narrow. "I hired him for a job. He's been helpful."

Bernard laughs. "Helpful. Yeah, that's Arthur." He looks over his shoulder again. "Look. I know we got off on the wrong foot, but I care about Arthur. We're close. I've known him since he joined up, and he's a good man. He just has one problem."

Shae can't help asking, just like he knows Bernard wants him to, "What is it?"

The last traces of humor fall from Bernard's face. He looks at Shae with the same disgust as when he first laid eyes on him in the inn. "He has terrible taste in men, and it's going to ruin his career." He stands up, towering over Shae. "If you care about him at all, and I think you do, well. Consider whether dragging him down is worth it."

He sweeps away, cloak billowing, before Shae can say anything in reply. Before Shae's heart stops racing, before his mind stops spinning. Because Bernard is an asshole, no doubt about that. But maybe he's not wrong about this.

Shae's still reeling when he hears Arthur's voice. He bolts from the mess tent to find Arthur outside the captain's tent, talking with her and Freya. He looks up immediately when he sees Shae.

"Are you done here?" Shae asks, ignoring the other paladins.

Arthur's smile is strained. "Hey, can we talk for a second?"

Shae's heart sinks. A thousand scenarios rush through his mind, and all of them boil down to this: now that Arthur has his fellow paladins, he doesn't want Shae anymore. Aware of the distrustful glares around him, Shae falls back on his usual mask of indifference. "Of course."

Arthur leads him towards their horses, tethered at the edge of camp. Duchess nuzzles Arthur's chest, and Sparrow continues grazing unconcerned. Shae feels like he's walking through an echoing dream, like there's a veil of anxiety between him and the ordinary world. He doesn't belong here. Arthur does.

"Is there any way we can stay here a couple days?" Arthur asks.

Shae's heart sinks further. It's not an outright rejection, but it doesn't need to be. He's not an idiot, and he can see where this is going. "I can't."

"Just a few days. Captain Tanner wants me to help capture Ronan." He takes Shae's hands and holds them. The sheer sun-bright heat of him floods into Shae's cold fingers. "My trial's at the end of the month, and it's not going to go well if I don't have something big to show for it."

Shae yanks his hands away. He can't think when Arthur's touching him. "What about banishing a demon? That seems pretty big to me."

"I asked Tanner about that. She said we could spare a few more men and women to ride north with you, once we have Ronan. How does that sound? Two days delay, and then we ride north with three times as much power."

Shae's hands are shaking. He crosses his arms and tries to hold himself still. "Do you really need to do this?"

Consider whether dragging him down is worth it.

Arthur looks him in the eyes. "My calling is everything. It's who I am," he says. "I need to make things right."

He's already gone, Shae realizes.

Even if he stays for a couple days, even if he stays for a month, he can't compete with Arthur's precious order. He can't handle staying and watching as Arthur draws further and further away. "Fine," he says coldly. "Good luck with that." He steps away to start untying Sparrow.

Arthur grabs his shoulder. "Wait, you need to stay here. You won't be able to—"

"Don't touch me," Shae snaps, jerking away. He takes a deep breath, striving to reach a cool, rational calm, because otherwise this won't work. He'll throw everything away and stay here with Arthur. "I'll hire someone else," he says, and doesn't try to keep the bitterness from his voice. "I don't need you *specifically.*"

"Shae," Arthur says quietly.

"It's just a job, right?" Shae laughs. He flips Sparrow's reins over his neck and starts digging through his coat pockets. Finding his coin purse, he counts out ten gold. "Here, this should cover what I owe you."

Arthur grimaces. "I don't need the money."

"Fine." Shae drops the coins on the ground. They clink together in the dirt. Fortunately, he manages to swing onto Sparrow's back on his first try, instead of faceplanting to the ground on top of the coins.

"If you insist on leaving, let me at least escort you back to town," Arthur says, reaching for Duchess's tether.

"If you follow me," Shae says, "I will kill you." He tugs Sparrow around and kicks him into a trot. Doesn't look back, just focuses on the road as it blurs in front of him. His eyes sting. With every jarring step, the warmth fades from his body, leaving his fingers cold around the reins.

There's no sound behind him. No final call, no pounding hooves of Arthur catching up. Shae tries to tell himself he isn't disappointed.

$$\text{)O(}$$

SHAE'S SPENT YEARS learning the limitations of his magic. Learning how long he can go without human contact. When his amber earring is fully charged with living aura, he can last nearly a day before the power is expended and he begins to truly hurt.

Lanwatch is only an hour's ride out of town, and Shae expects to reach the gate cold, but otherwise whole.

But only half an hour out of camp, knifelike chills slice through his lungs. He gasps, hands spasming, and the reins slip from his fingers. Sparrow comes to a halt, confused, as Shae hunches over, choking for breath. He braces himself on the horse's soft shoulders, barely feeling the rounded muscle beneath the coat. His fingertips already look faintly blue. It shouldn't be happening this fast, why—

Another pain arcs through him, like lightning coursing from his heart to his palms.

He grits his teeth, blinking through the sudden sparks in his eyes, and knows one more line of the array has broken. Izen is one step closer to freedom.

Ears still ringing with pain, Shae forces his numb fingers around the reins again and kicks. Sparrow takes one step forward, ears back and listening. No doubt wondering what the fuck his rider is doing, off-balance and trembling. The horse sets forward into a steady walk when Shae kicks again.

Shae's vision tunnels down to the dirt road before them and the points of Sparrow's ears twitching back and forth. He's halfway to town, and part of him desperately wants to turn around and race back to Arthur. He wants to soak in the warmth and safety he's never known anywhere else.

But Arthur isn't safe. Shae knew that from the start, and he shouldn't have forgotten it. Arthur's calling is more important to him than anything else. He was always just passing time with Shae, waiting for a reason to leave Shae behind. Even though he was kind. Even though he saw through Shae's defenses to the heart he wanted so badly to hide.

That connection was enough for Shae to drop his guard. But it wasn't enough to make Arthur stay.

Arthur would probably feel bad if he learned Shae died of cold in the middle of summer. Shae tries to derive a petty, ugly satisfaction from that, but it's hard to feel anything, bitter or sweet, as he keeps riding. Sparrow seems to move at a crawl, barely lifting each hoof as he walks forward. Shae wants to kick him faster, but he's afraid he'll fall off at the trot. He's swaying in the saddle as it is.

Sometime later—it feels like hours but it can't be that long—he senses a flicker of warmth ahead. Like a candle in a blizzard. Relief washes through his shivering limbs. Friend or foe, he doesn't care. He just needs someone.

Rounding a corner, he sees a group of people on horseback. One of them calls out, a voice he recognizes but can't quite place, "Necromancer?"

He opens his mouth to answer, but the words get lost before they reach his lips. The road and trees blur in front of him, and he slumps sideways in the saddle. He's unconscious before he hits the ground.

$$\supset\!O\!\subset$$

SHAE WAKES UP, bruised and aching but no longer freezing to death. He can feel his hands. They're cold, but cold is normal. He can deal with that. Even if he's gotten used to waking up in warm arms, with warm lips against his neck. Even if he's gotten weak to safety.

Keeping his breath steady, as if he's still asleep, he takes stock of his surroundings. He's lying down on something soft, fabric scratching his cheek, and sounds slowly filter into his awareness. A crackling fire before him. Voices behind him. Laughter. Rattling dice.

He recognizes the loudest voice. That Riverswords captain, Georgia Oakven.

Shae's eyes slit open, and he finds himself on a couch before a fireplace. The white walls are hung with broken swords and bows and axes. Trophies—though whether they belonged to the Riverswords members or their enemies, Shae doesn't know. He assumes he's in the Lanwatch outpost.

He sits up, hissing with pain as his left shoulder moves. He can't remember anything clearly, but he's pretty sure he fell off his horse. Nothing's broken, but he's going to be feeling the bruises for a while.

A rough male voice says, "Georgia, he's up."

"Thanks, darling," Georgia answers. Shae turns on the couch, not trusting his legs enough to stand yet, to see her drop a handful of dice on the wooden table. She grabs a tankard and walks over to Shae, winking when they make eye contact.

The men and women at the table resume their game, and Georgia perches on the arm of the couch. The firelight catches in her dark hair. "Sleep well, necromancer?"

Shae leans back against the cushions and prods his shoulder, seeking out the bruises. "Thanks for picking me up. I appreciate that."

"Just paying it forward." She sips from her tankard. "Reed here's picked me up off the side of the road enough times, I need to balance out my karma."

"You're *not* welcome," Reed calls from across the room. The others laugh.

Georgia flips him a rude gesture. "Besides, the information you gave last time was good. We slew three vaidkos outside the town graveyard, so thanks for that, now we're even," she tells Shae. "Your horse is in our yard. You're welcome to leave whenever you can walk out."

To the point, no unnecessary questions. She doesn't ask where his paladin friend is. She isn't friendly, but she doesn't hate him on sight either. This might be better, actually. Shae doesn't have the strength to deal with friendliness right now. All his focus has to be on his mission.

But he can't do it alone.

"Thanks," he says again. "Are you still under contract to hunt vaidkos?"

She cocks her head. "Aye."

Shae twists one of his rings. "I know where they're coming from," he says. "I can lead you to the source, in exchange for protection. But it's going to be dangerous"

Georgia eyes him up and down, then yells over her shoulder, "Reed, sweetheart, another ale over here!" She turns back to Shae and says, "Tell me more, darling. I'm all ears."

ARTHUR

Arthur doesn't watch Shae ride away, but every word of the conversation replays in his head. He can't figure out where it went wrong. He was so sure Shae would agree to stay, just for a couple of days. Shae has his own regrets—shouldn't he understand Arthur's need to absolve himself?

As he heads back into camp, he touches his pendant. The metal is cold.

Freya catches him before he gets to Tanner's tent. "The necromancer left?"

"He had business elsewhere," Arthur says.

"Probably for the best." She claps Arthur on the shoulder and grins at him, teeth bright against her brown skin. "It's good to have you back."

"It's good to be back," Arthur says, but the words feel hollow. They shouldn't. This is where he belongs, serving Vara's Radiance with his brothers and sisters in the order.

Bernard joins them. "Freya and I have the next patrol, and the captain said you should come with us."

"Perfect!" Freya says. "You can tell us everything you've been up to over the past year. I'm sure you've got stories."

His heart eases a little with their smiles. This is what he's missed—this warmth, this connection. He wants Shae here too, but Shae refused. That's not his fault. "Only if you catch me up on news from Ostaris," he says. "Did you ever get with that guardsman you were eyeing, Freya?"

Bernard bursts into laughter while Freya groans, covering her eyes in both hands. "There's nothing to say about that!" she protests.

"She forgot the guardsman," Bernard says, still laughing, "as soon as she met his *mother*."

"Radiance." Arthur can't help laughing with Bernard as Freya continues hiding behind her hands. "Yes, tell me everything."

☽○☾

THEY MOVE CAMP when the scouting party returns—two paladins Arthur knows from Ostaris, and a squire he doesn't recognize. With his freckled, heart-shaped face and messy auburn curls, the boy looks young, though he has to be at least eighteen to start training.

"Who's that?" Arthur asks, helping Bernard get his gear together. His own gear never got unpacked, and he needs something to do with his hands.

Bernard glances over. "The squire? That's Karis. He has tracking magic, among other things."

"Huh." Sure enough, there's a glint of blue and gold at the boy's earlobe. A focus gem. "Is that why they recruited him straight out of the cradle?"

Bernard chuckles. "Right? He joined up almost a year ago. I don't think he was even eighteen when he started. The Archpriest made an exception for him."

The more Arthur talks with Bernard and Freya and everyone else, the more he settles back into safe, familiar patterns. The process of packing up camp and setting out is routine. Tanner picks the two rearguard and calls for Freya to join her at the lead, and the rest fall into loose formation around the supply carts. Duchess ignores the other horses; she's always been more interested in humans, who are more likely to give her treats than steal them.

There's a chill in the air, and red and gold leaves mix in with the green canopy above. Bernard is off talking with someone else, and Arthur reins Duchess in until they fall back alongside Karis and his dapple gray mare.

"You're Karis, right?" Arthur says.

The boy looks over. His eyes are light amber, almost gold. "And you're Arthur Davorin." He has a slight accent Arthur can't quite place. "Did you need something?"

The strangest wave of recognition washes through Arthur, even though he's sure he's never met the squire before. Maybe the jewelry just reminds him of Shae. Or something about the way the boy carries himself.

"I heard you're our local tracking expert," Arthur says. "What do you need to have in order to find someone?"

He doesn't regret letting Shae go. He doesn't. This is where he belongs, in Vara's service with his brothers and sisters, and Shae is the one who refused to say. Arthur just wants to know that Shae's all right.

"Footprints help," Karis says with a smirk. "But if you mean magically, I need an item belonging to the person. I don't work for free, though, outside assignments."

"What do you charge?"

"Take my shift in the mess tent tomorrow night," the boy says immediately. "Sound fair?"

"Sure." Arthur reaches for his belt pouch, then stops. He doesn't have anything belonging to Shae. Just the coin that changed hands in previous weeks, but he knows enough about magic to know that won't work. Maybe he should have picked up the coins Shae threw at him this morning, instead of leaving them in the dirt for someone else to find. "What sort of item?"

Karis sighs. "Anything, as long as there's a connection. It doesn't have to actually belong to them, just has to be something they've touched recently enough." He glances sidelong at Arthur. "For Ronan Vizia, I've been using the knife he stabbed you with."

Arthur's hands tighten. Duchess tosses her head, annoyed, until he relaxes. "That's a little unnerving."

"A little," Karis agrees. "Who are you looking for? Is it the necromancer Stazie told me about?"

"His name is Shae," Arthur says, more sharply than he intended. The young squire doesn't seem offended, just smirks again. Arthur thinks a little longer, then loops his reins around the pommel and tugs off one of his gloves. "Here, he's touched this."

Karis takes his own gloves off, then nudges his mare a little closer to take the glove from Arthur. He sits back in the saddle, touches his earring, and closes his eyes.

A few seconds later, he lets go of his earring and hands the glove back.

"Did it not work?" Anxiety pools in Arthur's stomach. He'd expected something more, something flashier. Whispered words, or a shimmer of power through the air.

"Of course it worked," Karis says haughtily. "Your *friend* is in Lanwatch, with a pack of Riverswords, if I'm not mistaken." His grin widens. "And I'm never mistaken."

Riverswords. Of course.

"Thanks," Arthur says.

"Don't forget your kitchen shift tomorrow." Karis shakes his finger. He pulls his own gloves back on, then kicks his mare a bit faster, drawing ahead and leaving Arthur with too much space to think.

Shae was right. He found someone else, and he doesn't need Arthur after all. That should be reassuring. But the knot in Arthur's stomach doesn't go away.

)O(

AS THE SUN sinks over the ink-black treetops, Arthur steps away from camp to pray. He kneels in the soft, giving earth and bows his head towards the west, letting the last rays of daylight caress his head like the loving touch of Vara's hand. Not a parent but a teacher. A guide.

Arthur is in desperate need of guidance.

"Radiant Vara, brightest god," he murmurs, hands on his knees. He's spoken these words a hundred times, but now, they don't feel like ritual repetition. It's like he's speaking them new, straight from his heart on broken breath. "Grant your servant light, that I might see my path forward."

Behind him, the rest of camp laughs and clatters as they settle in for supper. He didn't have to walk a warding spell, because Freya and an older paladin had that duty tonight. When everyone picks up a piece, the burden is lighter.

Arthur continues, voice lowering even more, and his next words are no ritual at all. Just a plea: "Please, Vara, tell me I'm doing the right thing."

The sun sets, and Vara doesn't answer.

Arthur sleeps alone that night. He has a tent to himself, and he can't get warm. His hands itch to touch soft skin, caress bony arms and a narrow waist. His chest feels too light without Shae's head pillowed on it.

Dreams toss him back and forth in snatches of restless slumber until morning. He thinks it's another dream at first when someone taps the front of his tent, calling his name. Blearily, he gets up and unfastens the flap.

Freya's standing outside, her shirt untucked and excitement dancing in her eyes. "Get up, Arthur, no time to waste."

The sky is still the translucent gray before dawn. Behind Freya, sleep-deprived squires are saddling horses, including Duchess.

"What is it?" Arthur asks, immediately alert.

She grins. "We caught him."

Arthur's breath hitches. He doesn't have to ask who she's talking about.

SHAE

Dawn barely breaks over the eastern mountains as Shae and the Riverswords cross into Lyrisenia. There's no great change at the border. The heavy wooden city gate is already open, and the guards barely talk to Georgia before waving them through. Shae feels only the slightest tingle from the Northern Barrier.

A shiver still passes through Shae's bones at the crossing. He hasn't been this far north, this close to home, in nearly ten years. Not since he sold himself to Izen. Not since he said goodbye, again, to his parents.

Georgia rides at the front of the group on her flashy white horse, followed by Shae and six of her Riverswords. Her second in command, Reed, stayed behind in Lanwatch, and Shae's already forgotten the names of those accompanying them into Lyrisenia. He's too caught up in his own distractions. His whole body still aches from his fall the day before, and his thighs and back are sore from far more riding than he's used to. He hurts, and he's cold.

Even though it won't do anything, he tugs his coat closer around himself as he rides. He's not freezing. The Riverswords ride near enough that Shae can breathe in their living auras. But they're not close enough, their auras not bright enough, to keep him truly warm.

He used to be accustomed to this constant, low-level chill. But after a taste of true warmth, it's hard to go back to the cold.

Georgia brings the party to a halt a few miles out of Lanwatch. The road breaks off into four narrower paths, the forest encroaching on each of them. Evergreen trees pierce the sky, casting deep shadows. "Necromancer, now's a good time to pull out one of your parlor tricks. Find us the nearest nest of vaidkos."

Shae nudges Sparrow up next to Georgia's horse and loops the reins over the pommel. The gelding drops his head to pick at the weeds sprouting up in the middle of the road, disinclined to move if he doesn't have to.

"There's nothing within a mile of us, but I can amplify the spell." He takes the silver band from his right forefinger and holds it in his left first, then unsheathes his knife. "Give me a moment. And keep an eye on the horses, they don't always like this sort of magic."

"You heard him, sweethearts," Georgia tells her people.

Shae shoves his sleeve up his arm. His breath catches when he sees the most recently healed cuts. The ones

Arthur bandaged. Georgia eyes his movements with great interest, but no concern. That's good. Arthur's bleeding heart was patronizing. Annoying. Shae tells himself he doesn't miss the paladin's constant worry.

The blade kisses his skin in a thin line of blood. Shae resheathes the knife and presses his fingers to the cut, wetting them in blood so warm it tingles against his cold fingertips, and smears it on the ring. Blood still slides down his arm, ticklish and hot, as he murmurs in Lyrisenian, "Life's blood, lead me to darkness."

The ring vibrates in his palm, and he tightens his grip. It flashes painfully cold against his bare fingers, and it moves against him, pushing in a specific direction.

"There are vaidkos northeast of here," he says. "I'll let you know when we're a mile from them."

Georgia nods, and calls out, "This way, my dears." She trots forward, and the Riverswords fall into place around her.

Shae carefully works the ring back onto his finger, even as it keeps tugging northeast, then gathers his reins and kicks Sparrow to catch up. He doesn't stop to bandage his arm. The cut is shallow. It'll heal soon, and he can wash his shirt later. But a disproportionate amount of pain radiates from the injury, and he can't stop thinking about how tender Arthur's hands felt as he patched him up. The sense-memory of sweetness hurts more than the cut itself.

They break from the road as the forest thins around them, giving way to a broad crater of a valley. Shae knows the area as well as he knows any place in Lyrisenia. The Lyralan Crater is dotted with the remnants of a sprawling city and its castle, reduced to broken walls and exposed foundations by whatever disaster caused the crater long ago. The old cathedral, where Izen waits in the array, is north of it. The home Shae grew up in, where his parents rest, is to the east.

Every once in a while, Georgia asks him to confirm their direction. Shae's ring continues leading them through the rocky wasteland, unwavering in its direction. It leads them towards a jagged ruin silhouetted against the clear blue sky, until they don't need the ring anymore.

The screams ahead are plenty, and the flashes of black and red fire.

The Riverswords loosen their weapons without needing orders, some of them swearing over the sounds of hoofbeats. Georgia reins her horse in. "Here we go, darlings. Be ready to stop when we're in eyeshot, and I'll signal fight or flee when we see who's involved."

"*What's* involved," a woman with a blue armband says.

"Wait," Shae says, anxiety building. He wants to cast a few more spells, so they can see what's ahead without getting too close. But Georgia has already kicked her horse into a gallop, and her mercenaries follow without another word.

Swearing, Shae nudges Sparrow after them at a trot, as fast he can go without tumbling off the horse's back. Sparrow's ears prick forward, and he pulls against the bit, eager to follow the herd. As the Riverswords draw farther away, the cold begins to bite at Shae's hands and feet. They're a flash of white and bay in a plume of dark dust, heading towards a collection of broken walls and burning magic.

A horse screams, and someone yells. Hoofbeats clatter ahead, and a bay horse belonging to one of the Riverswords comes galloping back towards Shae, his rider nowhere to be seen. The horse shoots through the rocky landscape like an arrow, heedless of anything besides getting away.

Sparrow shies sideways as the riderless horse races past. The sudden movement knocks Shae's foot out of the stirrup. He swears, grabbing for mane and trying to rebalance, but he overcorrects. Time seems to stand still as he clings sideways to the saddle, his knee barely hooked over Sparrow's shoulder.

Then ground rushes towards him.

His thigh and shoulder take the brunt of the impact, and all the breath knocks from his lungs. He rolls away from Sparrow's hooves and springs to his feet, lunging for the reins, but the horse dances just out of reach. Shae can't catch the leather before Sparrow spins around and races away after the other horse.

"Fuck," Shae wheezes, clutching his shoulder. His breath comes back to him in painful heaves. Nothing feels broken, and the pain hasn't fully set in yet. He can push through the bruises.

Drawing his knife, he staggers towards the dark magic and screams ahead.

He walks into a bloodbath. Men and women and monsters fight in the shadow of a broken tower, surrounded by the remains of an ancient curtain wall and the wreckage of a far more recent camp. There are crumpled tents and still-smoldering cookfire embers scattered beneath the combatants' feet.

There are bodies on the ground, too. Not River-swords. They might be bandits, like the ones that killed his parents, but Shae can't dredge up any anger right now. His stomach is too sick with the scent of blood, the sight of bone breaking through limbs.

One of the Riverswords gallops past him, nearly knocking him over as she rides away from the carnage. A vaidkos leaps from a crumbled stone wall and slams into her, clawing her to the ground. Her scream breaks off when the vaidkos's jaws tear through her throat. Blood sprays into the air, painting her skin and clothes, including her blue armband.

Shae throws himself into the wall's shadow and peers around it, trying to see what's happening. Georgia and two of her people are fighting vaidkos and human corpses alike. The vaidkos wield fangs and claws, and the corpses wield spears and axes and knives—

And teeth as well. One lunges for Georgia, teeth bared, and nearly bites her before she shoves her sword down its throat. A scream rattles from its dead body, and she kicks it off her sword.

None of them see Shae yet. His warding rings are still working, but it's only a matter of time. There are too many vaidkos and corpses, and too few mercenaries. Guilt seizes Shae in iron claws. He shouldn't have brought these people out here. This was his mistake to clean up, but all he's doing is getting people killed.

He needs to do something.

Anything.

As soon as the vaidkos lunges away, Shae darts for the woman with the armband. He falls to his knees beside her and whispers, "Sorry," as he splays his hand over her mangled chest. His fingers sink into the wounds, and he feels wet bone against his palm. Her throat is gone, but her face is intact, with dead eyes and slack jaw. She was blond and pretty. Shae doesn't remember her name, and he fixates on that instead of the gore slipping through his fingers.

With a shuddering breath, he lets in the darkness. Power rushes into him like a river of dark fire, and the pain and violence and resentment of the mercenary's death floods into him. As much as he can take without losing himself. The shadow and light cage shivers around his innermost soul, close to fracturing. Shae takes in as much as he dares, and then a little more, and then searches for a target.

He draws the dead energy like a bowstring, and releases it.

The power arcs through air and slams into the vaidkos fighting Georgia. The lizard-like creature screeches and tumbles sideways, running into one of its brethren. Georgia lunges forward and hacks at its neck, sending up a plume of green-black blood.

Shae turns his attention to the next target, and the next. A rotting farmer's head explodes with Shae's stolen power, but it's too late to save the gutted mercenary falling to his knees beside him. Shae doesn't pay attention to him. He can't help the wounded; his magic doesn't heal. All he can do is kill, and take from the dead.

"Nightven!" Georgia screams from across the wrecked camp, just as every ring on his right hand *burns*.

His concentration breaks, and the next arc of power shatters around him. He barely throws himself to the side before a black sword sinks into the earth where he was kneeling. The hem of his coat tears around the blade. Agony ripping through his hand, Shae scrambles to his feet.

A figure in dark clothing stands above the woman with the armband. With his tattered brown coat and black trousers, he's dressed just like the other dead bandits scattered across the campsite. Long, blood-matted hair covers most of his waxy, pale face. Both his arms hang by his side. The black blade lifts of its own accord and hovers beside him. The corpse lifts his head, and familiar red eyes bore into Shae.

Shae throws the arrow of death energy, but Izen's sword spins around and deflects it. Izen walks forward, stepping on the blond mercenary's body as he crosses it. The ring on Shae's right forefinger blazes once more, then goes inert, its power spent.

"Shaesarenna." Izen's voice is hoarse through the dead man's throat. "You're getting better at this. I thought you'd always be too scared to truly use the gift I gave you."

"A gift?" Shae snaps. "I paid plenty for this." He backs up slowly, casting around for a better weapon. Another source of power. There are two dead bandits slumped against the wall, if he can get to them—

He lunges, but only gets a few steps before a cold hand slams around his throat. Izen is a blur of dark movement. He forces Shae back against the wall, the crumbled top of it hitting just below his shoulder-blades. Shae curves back against the stone, the dead man's hand like an iron collar. Cold permeates his entire body. He wishes desperately, pathetically, for

Arthur's heat, Arthur's touch. The comfort of Arthur's mere voice, to get him through this.

Izen reeks of blood and death. The full, cold weight of the corpse he wears presses against Shae's body. The intimacy crawls down Shae's spine, more sickening than the reek of death. There's no warmth in the touch. None of the relief that usually comes from human contact.

"You can't kill me," Shae wheezes. "Or you'll go back to the realm you came from."

"I can kill all your little friends, though," Izen says with a wet, coughing laugh. The dead man's face spreads in a horrible grin. "All these delicious souls you brought for me to devour."

Shae's stomach drops. He can't see if anyone else is still standing. He can't hear anything besides the terrified pounding of his own heart.

"And I can do this." Izen's eyes flash red, and he leans forward. The corpse's cold lips press against Shae's.

He freezes, too shocked to struggle. Bile rises in his throat. An awful, cold tongue nudges against the seam of his lips for a moment that lasts far too long.

Then he can't feel the kiss, because pain recoils through him. Sharp. Cold. A door slamming inward, a window shattering outward. His ears ring with the crackle of power. The jagged edges of a broken spell. His knees buckle, and only the grip on his throat keeps him upright.

The array is gone. Izen is free.

The demon laughs against his lips, a horrible rattling sound, and draws away. His hand loosens around Shae's throat, and he hisses something Shae doesn't understand. Eyes burning red, he lifts his face towards the sky.

"I'll be back for you, Shaesarenna," Izen says gleefully, before the corpse he wears crumples to the ground. A whirlwind of shadows bursts from it and races away into the sky.

Shae's ears are still ringing. He can't hear anything else as he collapses beside the corpse.

ARTHUR

The scouting party commandeered a local farmer's barn to hold Ronan. Arthur swings from Duchess's saddle as soon as they reach it. The ride was quick, but Arthur's too warm under his tunic. His hand itches for his sword. He leaves it sheathed at his saddle, so he doesn't do something he'll regret.

The sun barely crests the treetops, and the early sunbeams break through the branches as if through the windows of the Bright Cathedral. The barn was once painted blue, but now only flecks of color remain against the gray wood. Doors on each side open from stalls into animal pens, with pigs on one side and goats on the other. Behind the barn, the small plot of land is lush green, nearly ready for harvest. There are three horses already tied to the fence, and Karis the squire waits near them. He darts to Captain Tanner as she dismounts.

"Stazie and Harry have him inside." Karis adds, as if he'd forgotten, "Sir."

Arthur expects Tanner to bark at the boy for the disrespect, but she doesn't seem to notice. "Excellent work." She turns to the rest of them—Arthur, Freya, and Bernard. "You lot stand guard out here. Arthur, I'm sure you have a lot to say to Vizia. I'll call you in a minute."

"Yes, sir," he says, and watches her stiff, straight back disappear into the barn. He tethers Duchess with the other horses, checking her tack just to have something to do with his hands.

He doesn't actually have a lot to say to Ronan Vizia.

He's so close to finally being able to ask *why*, but something feels off. Disappointing. Tanner asked him to stay to help catch Ronan, but he hasn't actually done anything. He was asleep while an eighteen-year-old kid found Ronan overnight. Not exactly the heroic redemption Arthur was offered.

He pats Duchess's neck and joins Bernard at the tree line.

"Why the long face?" Either Bernard is more perceptive than usual, or Arthur's mood is just that obvious.

"It just feels a little weird," Arthur says. "I've spent all year running around on my own, wondering what Ronan is doing. And now I'm here with you guys, and Ronan's been captured, and it's almost all over."

Bernard laughs. "How is that weird? I thought you'd be thrilled about all this."

Arthur rubs his chin and stares out into the brightening forest. He remembers how it felt to wake up alone. "I thought so too," he says quietly. "I don't know.

Maybe it just feels wrong that I had to break a contract to stay here."

"A contract?" Bernard laughs again, far too loudly for the serene stillness of the morning. "How bad did that corpse-fucker mess with your head? You don't need to honor—"

Arthur punches him.

He doesn't realize what he's doing until Bernard is already staggering back, covering his nose.

"Radiance, what the fuck?" Blood trickles past the man's fingers.

Arthur stares as if seeing Bernard for the first time. He remembers walking into the inn at Lanwatch and seeing Bernard and Shae facing off. He remembers the way Bernard laughed and explained everything away, but Shae never stopped glaring. Of course he didn't. Shae was in danger, and instead of defending him, Arthur invited the threat to their table.

No wonder Shae left to find a new set of bodyguards. Shae hired Arthur to protect him—worse, Shae trusted him—and Arthur let him down.

"Shae's a good man," Arthur says, staring Bernard in the eyes. "A better man than me."

"Radiance." Bernard prods his nose and winces. "I won't tell Tanner about this, because of our abiding *friendship*, but you need to get your head on straight."

"Go ahead and tell her," Arthur says, far more calmly than he feels. "And if I hear another insult about Shae, I'll punch you again."

Freya rushes over. "What are you idiots doing?" She pulls Bernard's hand away from his nose. "Arthur, what's—"

Arthur ignores them both and stalks towards the barn. Bernard can tell Freya his side of the story. Arthur cares less and less what his friends think of him with every passing second.

The barn door is closed. Karis leans next to it, arms crossed, watching Arthur with interest. "You're a lot more fun than I expected," he says when Arthur stops at the door.

Arthur turns towards him. The boy looks so young. Did Arthur look like this when he first joined? Young and excited and eager to learn swords and magic and following orders? He wanted to be a paladin of Vara since he was old enough to ask his father who the people with the sunny coats were. But the sun on his tunic wasn't the reason he joined. The magic, the uniform, the hierarchy, the law, even the friends, they were all a means to an end.

"Why did you join the order, Karis?" he asks.

"The same as everyone," Karis says loftily. "To serve the Radiant and defend the helpless."

"That's what I wanted too." Arthur squints up at the rising sun through the trees. "But I can't do that here."

After a moment, Karis prompts, "Sir?"

Arthur ignores him too and pushes the door open.

The barn is brightly lit, with the outer stall doors all open to let the animals outside for the day. The stench is overpowering for the first few breaths, and then everything falls away when he sees Captain Tanner, Stazie, and Harry standing over a bound, kneeling figure.

"Captain," Arthur says from the open door.

She whips around and frowns. "You can talk to him in a minute. Wait outside."

Her movement gives Arthur his first clear view of Ronan in nearly a year.

Even bound and kneeling, covered in grime, Ronan is handsome. His bronze skin gleams in the torchlight, and the chains around his arms only emphasize their heft. There's a streak of blood drying on his high cheekbone. He looks relaxed despite the circumstances. When he sees Arthur, his lip twitches, but he says nothing and quickly returns to his impassive mask. There's no trace of the smile Arthur fell in love with.

"Hello, Arthur," Ronan says, coolly.

Arthur realizes he has nothing to say in return.

All this ruminating, all this wondering why, doesn't matter anymore. No explanation Ronan gives can change what he's done to Arthur. It won't make Arthur feel better. It won't bring the Crown of Vara back. It won't bring the priest he killed back.

There's nothing Ronan can say that Arthur wants to stand here and listen to, when he should be fulfilling the truth purpose of his oath. Sharing light. Helping people. His faith is deeper than orders and ranks and politics. Right now, he needs to help a lonely, prickly necromancer. Any of his brothers and sisters can do what's needed in the order. They can escort Ronan back to the Bright Cathedral and put him to trial without Arthur, easily. But only Arthur can help Shae, because he's the only one who wants to.

He thinks Vara will understand.

"I'm not here to talk to him, sir," Arthur says, facing Tanner squarely. "I wanted to tell you I'm leaving. My penance isn't over, and you don't need me here. You have him." He gestures at Ronan.

"Now's not the time," she says. "Wait outside, and we'll talk about this when I'm done in here."

"No," Arthur says. He hears a whistle from Stazie, and rustling as the others shift, but keeps his gaze firmly on the captain he's disobeying for the first time in his life.

Tanner crosses her arms. "Don't worry about the trial. I'll find you another task that looks good for it. Unless I change my mind because you're being insubordinate."

Before, the stern tone in her voice would have snapped him to attention. Now, he doesn't care. Redemption isn't about appearances. "I'm not worried about the trial," he says. "I have something more important to take care of."

He turns around. Not all of his long-engrained reflexes are gone yet; he still stops near the door when Tanner barks, "Davorin!"

He looks over his shoulder. "Yes, sir?"

"Are you running off to that necromancer?"

"His name is Shae," Arthur says. "And yes."

"I just want you to know, I'll be honor-bound to testify about this at your trial," she says. "If you leave for him now, the Archpriest will never let you back in."

Arthur pulls his pendant from under his shirt. He looks at the golden sun he's carried for five years. But his purpose is more than a symbol. If he can't bring Vara's magic, then so be it. He'll give Shae his heart and his sword if those are all he has.

He pulls the chain over his head and drops it to the ground. The small noise seems to thunder through the dusty, smelly barn. Arthur's never seen Captain Tanner surprised before.

"Then I quit," he says. "Light guide you."

He walks out before anyone can reply.

Karis is waiting just outside the door, eyes wide. Arthur walks past him, then remembers something and whirls around to grab his shoulder. "Track Shae again," he says roughly. "Tell me where he is."

The boy's jaw drops, then clicks shut. Divine power flickers through him, tingling Arthur's hand where they touch. Karis's brow furrows, and then he opens his eyes again. "About seven miles northeast of Lanwatch," he says. "A ruin in the Lyralan Crater."

Moments later, Arthur's up in the saddle, kicking Duchess toward the road. Bernard shouts something after him, but he neither understands nor cares what he's saying. All Arthur knows is the pounding of galloping hooves, Duchess moving beneath him, the wind whipping past him—and a strange, exhilarating feeling rising within him.

He thinks it's the adrenaline at first. The shock of turning his back on everything he thought he wanted burning deep in his chest, driving him forward. The sensation surges, cresting into white-hot illumination. Sunlight floods him, and for a moment, everything he sees—road, trees, skyline—is limned in golden light. The brilliance stings his eyes to the edge of tears.

On his next blink, the world returns to normal, and the light settles into his heart, a steady, reassuring power. He thought that throwing away his pendant would break his connection to Vara's power. Instead, his magic feels stronger than ever before, and he has the guidance he's prayed for: Vara's Radiance, spurring him forward.

He's doing the right thing. He just hopes it's not too late.

SHAE

The earth is dark and wet beneath Shae when he gasps awake. Death fills his lungs, so thick he chokes on it. He scrambles to his knees so fast that the blood rushes from his head, and he slumps sideways again. His hands are numb. His wrists barely support his weight as he sits again more slowly.

Gray light filters through the clouds above. It's impossible to tell what time it is. Corpses surround him. Riverswords and bandits, and gods only know what else. The older corpses that Izen dragged to fight. Ashes of dead vaidkos mingle with the bloodstained dirt. Shae's stomach seizes, and he breathes through the nausea until it subsides.

Standing up takes longer than it should. He falls again to one knee. Counts his breaths. Touches a stud in his right ear for a quick burst of strength that finally gets him upright. He barely feels the magic as he uses it. That's how he knows he's really, truly cold.

He drags himself around the wreckage and checks each fallen body for life. It's useless, he knows it's useless, but he has to. None of them have any breath left in them. A couple of the Riverswords feel warm to the touch, but Shae doesn't know what that really means. He's so cold himself that the newly dead bodies would naturally be warmer than him.

He counts six Riverswords. Two men and four women—almost all the ones who rode into Lyrisenia with him. Only Georgia is missing. She must have gotten away, leaving Shae alone on the bloody ground. He's too numb to be mad about that. Running away was the smart thing to do. None of them were any match for Izen with the array this weak.

Shae's still no match for him. Not in this condition. Maybe not ever. He laughs sharply in the middle of the spread of bodies. He thought he learned the lesson of hubris when he was twelve years old—that wanting something with every bone in his body doesn't mean he can have it. But no. Once again his recklessness has consequences.

Just as well he left Arthur behind. Maybe the paladin's magic could have made a difference, or maybe Arthur could be lying lifeless in the dirt too.

Shae can't help missing him, with a fully-body ache that rivals the cold.

He lifts his hands. His fingertips look blue already, and he needs to find people fast. But the nearest settlement is too far away, and he doesn't remember exactly how to get there. He definitely won't make it back to Lanwatch on foot. He'll die before then.

Shae kneels beside a dead bandit. The man is older, with a patch over his eye and blood in his scraggly gray beard. Shae doesn't know if he was a good man or a bad man. The sort of man that rode through the Nightven homestead and killed Shae's parents, or just a hungry man trying to get by. Maybe both, or neither. He's not good or bad now, just dead.

And the violence and fear of his death wait in the shadows of his soul, ripe for the plucking. All the bodies around him are a source of power too. If Shae wants to banish Izen, if he wants to end all this and get rid of his necromancy for good?

He can't fix anything if he's dead. Whatever the risk, he has to take it.

Hands shaking, Shae unfastens the silver feather from his right lobe. Drops it on the ground next to the one-eyed bandit's corpse. It's easier than Shae thought it would be. The last protective wall crumbles from his soul with barely a whisper of sensation.

Shae covers the dead man's mouth with his palm, and closes his eyes.

No words. No apology, no incantation. He doesn't feel sorry, and he doesn't need to beg. The power floods into him immediately, eager and desperate for the slightest invitation, and Shae welcomes it just as desperately. The darkness is a rushing river. His breath hitches. His eyes fly open but see nothing as the dark power surrounds and fills him.

It doesn't hurt. Nothing hurts. Shae breathes in the shadows and calls to the other corpses. The last remnants of power inside them rush towards him too. Intoxicating. He should have done this years ago.

When the corpses are empty, Shae rises to his feet. He opens his mouth to thank them, then laughs. They're dead. They don't matter. They were only tools to feed his strength, and now they're not even that.

He can't feel anything. No pain, no fear, no sorrow. No warmth, but no cold. He can survive like this. But is it enough? The only thing he feels is a new, dark hunger crawling through his body. He needs to be strong to face Izen. Surely more power would be safer.

A memory surfaces. A little homestead, at the far eastern edge of the Lyralan Crater. The memory should hurt, but it doesn't now. All that matters is the two graves behind the house. Perhaps he can take one last gift from them, as recompense for leaving him.

)O(

WHEN SHAE REACHES his childhood home, the memories feel like they belong to someone else. He's not the boy who lived in the single-story stone building. He's not the boy whose mother patched the walls with magic, or whose father thatched the roof with his own two hands. He's not the boy who drew water from the well out front, or threw pebbles down it to see how long they fell before they splashed.

His father held some other boy on his shoulders to pluck the fruit from the trees behind the house. His mother showed some other boy how to darn the holes in his socks.

Another boy ran as far south as he could, another man kept running and running, for fear of angering the dead, for fear of drowning in sorrow like a pebble sinking into water. Another. Not Shae, who feels nothing besides hunger.

The dreamlike haze carries him to the orchard behind the house. The trees are still black and twisted from his last visit home. Some of them have fallen, tangles of twisted branches without leaves or fruit, their roots exposed and dead. At the center of the dead grove rest two gray stones. There are no words on them.

Shae stands above his parents' graves. "You left me," he says quietly. "And you refused to come back when I needed you. So I'm not asking this time."

Another thought briefly crosses his mind. Why does he need to banish Izen now? He's not afraid of the power anymore. He feels so much better now that he's given in. Maybe he should kill Izen instead, to make sure nobody else can ever banish him and rob Shae of his newfound strength. Or he could join with Izen, work together to become even more powerful, consume even more, and kill anyone who ever tries to stop them.

Shae laughs. Whichever path he decides, he needs this power.

He draws his knife. But before he can slice open his arm, the sound of hoofbeats thunders from the west.

ARTHUR

rthur sees three horses ahead just north of the border. He urges Duchess faster to intercept them. He recognizes two of them: Georgia Oakven's flashy white steed, and the little dark bay gelding he helped Shae buy just the morning before.

None of the horses have riders. They whip past Arthur and Duchess, eyes wide and ears pinned back, racing for the safety of the Lanwatch gate. Arthur sees a streak of blood across the white horse's flank as it passes.

Duchess shies under him, but quickly calms as Arthur nudges her into a canter. Arthur wishes he had her composure. It's all he can do to keep his hands steady on the reins.

He's never been north of the border before, and all he has to go on are vague memories of maps and the directions from Karis. Seven miles northeast of

Lanwatch. But Vara's Radiance hasn't left him, even without a focus item. Whenever he turns the wrong direction, whether through confusion or a turn in the road, the warmth inside him fades. It surges like wildfire when he's on the right path again.

As the trees thin out and the scope of the Lyralan Crater spreads around him, a needle-prick of darkness pierces his awareness. Evil whispers in the same direction that Vara's Radiance guides him. Arthur doesn't know if it's vaidkos or demon or walking corpse. He just knows he has to keep going.

He might have missed the tower remnants were it not for the ravens. The ruins are just north of his path. But the cawing cries and fluttering wings attract his attention. He rides closer in and sees the first broken body. A woman with her throat torn out, a raven pecking at her stomach, and a Riverswords-blue armband. The rest of the bodies spread out behind her.

Arthur dismounts, shoving away his nausea and fear, and checks for survivors. There are none, but something selfish and scared inside him eases when he finishes looking through them and hasn't found Shae.

Wherever Shae is, it's not on the bloody ground here.

The fallen deserve to rest in peace, buried or burned to return to the earth and sky. Arthur can't give them that now. All he can do is touch his heart and murmur, "May Vara's Radiance light your way."

He mounts up again and rides east, pushed by Vara's Radiance towards the whispering darkness.

His destination appears at the edge of the crater. A lone farmhouse, dilapidated but not completely ruined like the other buildings he's seen so far in Lyrisenia.

There are holes in the roof, and the windows are broken. A chicken coop sits empty in the front.

Vara's Radiance flares inside him, then goes dark, and Arthur knows he's in the right place. Uneasy pressure fills his ears, like he's climbed too high a mountain. His skin crawls, and the air is too cold in his lungs. There's something evil behind the house. He gallops forward, Duchess's gait never faltering beneath him. She only stops when he reins her in sharply at the sight ahead.

At the center of a blackened orchard kneels a solitary figure. A plume of shadows twists above, rising like smoke through the skeletal branches. Two dark gray stones sit in front of him.

Arthur swings from the saddle and unsheathes his sword. He still can't identify the source of the darkness he feels, pressing into his awareness like the edge of a knife not quite breaking the skin. But he recognizes, with an even stronger pang, the figure before him.

"Shae!" he shouts, running forward. "Get over here!"

He needs Shae to get away from the shadows. Away from danger. Forgetting he threw his pendant away, Arthur presses his hand to his chest. All he touches is tunic and leather armor, but golden light still comes to his call. The rays burst from him, intended to form a protective shield—

But they dissipate in a circle around Shae's kneeling figure, and Shae doesn't move.

Were it not for the sick tension humming through the air, the necromancer would look peaceful. Reverent. His pose is very like that of prayer.

Arthur stops short, ten feet away, sensing something wrong. "Shae," he says hoarsely. "What's going on?"

Shae's body shakes. Trembles. A wheezing sound breaks the silence of the orchard, growing louder with each second, until it heightens into peals of harsh laughter. The sound grates in Arthur's ears. Still laughing, Shae jerks to his feet and turns around.

He looks far too pale, the skin under his eyes bruised with exhaustion. He's nearly skeletal, his bones ready to break through his paper-thin skin. Bruises mottle his neck. His eyes flicker black, then gray again. The shadows aren't just surrounding him. They're rising from his body. He's the source.

"Shae, what have you done?"

"What I had to," Shae rasps. "I gave my soul to the power, and it's too late to turn back. So, fuck off if you know what's good for you."

Arthur's heart pounds in his throat. His ears are about to pop from the pressure. He adjusts his grip on his sword. "I'm not fucking off this time."

Shae laughs again. "Suit yourself, paladin."

That's the only warning before knife-like shadows arc around him and streak towards Arthur's heart.

"Radiance," Arthur swears and prays, and dodges.

He swings his sword up to deflect the shadows, and the blade shimmers golden with Vara's gift. The shadows hiss as they collide with the steel, then ricochet back. Arthur lunges sideways to dodge the next volley, severing a handful of shadows in midair. They dissipate. More stab towards him in their stead.

Shae remains still as ice throughout, a statue in the midst of roiling shadows. Only his face gives any indication of life—sick amusement crumpling into rage.

That anger gives Arthur hope. He refuses to believe he's too late.

"I'm sorry," Arthur says, parrying another blow. He sidesteps the next strike from behind. "I should have left with you."

Shae lifts his chin. "That doesn't matter now."

Arthur can fix this. He has to be able to fix this. He just needs an opportunity to get close to Shae without getting skewered first. "I'm serious. The order didn't need me. I wanted them to need me, but they didn't. I shouldn't have let you go alone."

"How noble," Shae spits. His face twists with rage, and the next shadow launches past Arthur's blade, punching into his left shoulder. The leather armor can't deflect it, and the skin splits. "But I don't need you either. Your righteous charity isn't required."

Arthur's shoulder burns with cold, then the heat of blood, but he doesn't dare take his eyes off Shae to look at it. "I'm sorry."

"I don't care."

"Then why are you so angry?" Arthur sees the slightest flinch in the stony face. "I think you still care. I think you want me to help you."

"*I don't care*," Shae hisses again. But the frozen statue fractures. When Arthur steps forward, he steps back.

The shadow knives dart towards Arthur, and he can't deflect all of them. He pushes forward anyway, praying silently, and the light flares around his blade, buying him another second. He has one chance to save Shae. The cleansing spell will take all his strength, and if he fails, he knows that Shae will kill him before he recovers.

He's not afraid of dying. He just hates the thought of what that would do to Shae, if he ever wakes up from this madness on his own.

"Let me help you," Arthur says. Takes a deep breath. "I love you."

Shae's eyes widen for a split second, then darken wholly black. Arthur takes the single moment of surprise to throw his sword aside. If he fails, he won't need his sword anyway. He seizes Shae by the shoulder, by the back of his head. Feels the trembling resistance to his touch and ignores it, tangling his fingers in Shae's hair.

"I'll kill you," Shae snarls as Arthur presses his lips to his forehead.

Shae's cooler to the touch than he's ever been. Arthur's entire consciousness centers around a single, simple prayer: *Help him.*

Vara's answer isn't light or heat. Arthur's not even sure the power comes from Vara. It's a surge of emotion from the depths of his heart. Memories rush through him. The way Shae snapped at him that morning in the Moon's Barrel. His smile at Duchess, barely an hour later. Touching his thigh to reposition him in the saddle. The serious look on his face at the Harvest Lord graveyard, insisting on covering a dead woman's grave. The way he never flinched when cutting open his own arm, but flew to Arthur's side after the vaidkos ambush.

Shadows slice into his arms and shoulders, trying to pull him away. They don't dig as deep as they could. They don't go for Arthur's throat. Even now, Shae isn't trying to truly kill him.

Arthur holds fast to the thin, trembling body in his arms. He remembers the Harvest Lord's graveyard again, pulling Shae close after, warming him up with his own body. Arthur sticks on that memory, more than anything that came after. The kissing, the sex, the smiles—he loves that, he wants that, but what truly matters is holding Shae. Giving up as much of his own heat, his own life force, as Shae needs.

Shae's breath is ragged now. Shadow-cold claws loosen around Arthur's arms.

"I love you," Arthur murmurs again into Shae's cold skin, and he feels the moment when Shae breaks.

He falls against Arthur, panting and trembling. The last of the shadows wither into nothing, and the dead orchard brightens almost imperceptibly around them.

SHAE

rthur's arms are the only thing keeping Shae upright. The cold and dark seep away, leaving only emptiness in their wake. All he can do is gasp for breath and clutch Arthur's tunic, shaking.

The first thing that fills that emptiness is warmth. More than the paladin's aura, more than the simple warmth of human touch. It's a surge of emotion. Relief, need, euphoria. Something more. A small, scared part of his soul no longer alone.

The second thing is pain. Shae winces, fists tightening. His entire body feels like—well, he feels like he fell off a horse a few times, got strangled by dead people, and walked a few frozen miles to his parents' graves. Even the pain is welcome. It's such a relief to feel anything again.

The rest of the memories flood back in. Losing control of the darkness, losing control of himself.

Trying to kill Arthur, because Shae could take his energy afterwards, because Arthur had the gall to interfere before Shae could siphon out the last remnants of his parents.

He breathes into Arthur's collarbone, "You came back."

Arthur's hand loosens in Shae's hair and slides down between his shoulderblades. "Yeah."

"Did you—" He flashes back to their conversation outside the paladins' camp. "Did you already get what you needed from Ronan?"

"I didn't need anything from Ronan," Arthur says into his hair. "I shouldn't have let you go alone. I'm sorry."

Shae inhales, unclenches his fists with effort, and drapes his arms over Arthur's shoulders. "I think I'm still mad at you."

Arthur laughs breathlessly and hugs Shae closer. "That's fine. You can be mad."

"Thanks," Shae says dazedly. "I appreciate that."

He's steady enough to stand on his own now, and part of him wants to. He's ashamed and scared by how close he came to killing Arthur. How close he came to reprising his greatest regret and disturbing his parents' rest once again. He wants to hide from any judgment of Arthur's.

The rest of him wants to stay here forever, selfishly savoring the man's touch.

None of that matters now, though. The array is gone. Shae has no idea what Izen will do next, but it can't be good. He extricates himself reluctantly from the embrace. "The array broke," he says urgently. Remembering *how* it broke, he shudders at the memory of cold lips on his. "Izen's free, I don't know where he'll go next, I need—you're hurt."

Blood pours from a too-long, too-deep gash in Arthur's left arm. From other wounds too, tearing through Arthur's leather armor, staining his sun-emblazoned tunic. Dizziness sweeps through Shae.

I did that.

Arthur doesn't look down at his injuries. He catches Shae by the elbow, as if Shae's the injured one. "It's nothing serious. Tell me about Izen." He looks down at his arm, tries to move it, and winces. "Okay, that one might need stitches."

Shae swallows down his distress and wordlessly leads Arthur out of the dead orchard.

There's a medical kit in Arthur's saddlebags. Shae sits Arthur down at the edge of the well and draws up water to wash off his wounds. The well hasn't run dry in the years since he last came here. He feels Arthur's gaze on him as he works the handle, which creaks with every movement. The rope is frayed, but somehow still intact.

"Was this your home?" Arthur asks quietly.

Shae rests the bucket of water on the edge of the well, gripping the edge of the bucket so tightly that his knuckles turn white under his rings. "Yes." He forces himself to let go. "Do you have a spare shirt I could ruin?"

Arthur hesitates, then yanks his sun-blazoned tunic from under his belt and pulls it over his head. "Here."

Shae takes it hesitantly. "I'm serious about ruining it. Don't you..."

"I don't need it," Arthur says calmly. His stubbled jaw visibly tightens, then relaxes.

There's something more hiding under his words, but if Arthur doesn't want to talk, Shae doesn't have the right to ask. His first priority is patching up the injuries he caused. As if that will make it any better. He draws his knife and splits the tunic in half, then starts using one of the pieces as a towel to sponge the blood from Arthur's cuts.

He moves slowly, methodically. He doesn't flinch when Arthur asks, "What happened to the orchard behind the house?"

"I did," Shae answers quietly. He half-kneels on the side of the well to get a better angle to clean the cuts on Arthur's back. They're shallow. The leather armor blunted the worst of it. "I told you I tried to revive my parents."

Arthur hisses in pain, but doesn't move away. "Yes."

"And I told you it didn't work." Shae moves to the deeper cut in Arthur's left arm, high up by the shoulders. He hesitates, then grabs his knife again to widen the tear in the sleeve, to give himself more room to work. "I lied about it not working."

Arthur exhales sharply. "Radiance, Shae."

"I had already buried them, and I had to dig them up again. I sat them up against the tree in the middle of the orchard, so they wouldn't have to wake up in their graves. My father's favorite tree." He takes his time cleaning out the cut, pausing every time Arthur flinches. It starts to bleed sluggishly again, and he wipes away the fresh blood too. "They'd been dead for a month at the time. It took me that long to summon Izen, and to learn enough magic from him. So, Mom and Dad had already started to rot."

Arthur hands Shae the needle, thread, and denseed oil. "Have you stitched a wound before?"

"Yes. But you should probably see an actual healer when you have a chance." Shae dabs some oil into the cut to prevent infection, then threads the needle. Continues talking, because if he doesn't finish now, he never will, and somehow he feels he has to. "It took me three tries to get the resurrection spell right. It finally worked at sunset, and the force of the spell killed the entire orchard. But I didn't care about the orchard, because Mom and Dad woke up."

He pulls the edges of the wound together and starts the first stitch. It's easier to talk about this when he's doing something. It's easier to do this when he's talking about something.

"I was worried they wouldn't come back right, but they did. It was them. They knew themselves. They knew me. I was so happy to have them back."

Arthur stays still and silent as Shae continues stitching and talking.

"But they weren't happy." Shae takes a deep breath, waiting for his eyes to clear before making the next stitch. "The first thing Mom said when she woke up was, 'Send us back.'" He can hear her voice as clearly as if she stood here now. "They were angry. They wanted to rest. But I refused to break the spell."

The stitches are done. He cuts off the thread and places the needle back in its case. Arthur takes it from him without speaking.

"Mom was a hedgewitch, and she still had her own magic," Shae says quietly. "She burned out Dad's heart, then her own, so they could die again. I buried them, then left." He can still smell the dead flesh burning. Suddenly unable to sit still, he stands up.

But Arthur stands up too, seizing his hands. Running his thumbs over his rings. "You still blame yourself," he says slowly.

"Of course." Shae's eyes sting. "It was my fault. I hurt them because I was selfish."

"Can you feel them here?" Arthur asks, pulling him a little closer.

"What?"

Arthur squeezes his hands. "Do any of your rings detect anything?"

His touch is so safe and comforting, even though Shae doesn't deserve it. He tries to pull his hands away, but Arthur holds him fast. "No. I don't feel them. Is that supposed to—"

"Then they're at peace now." Arthur looks down at him, an impossibly soft expression in his green eyes. "There are no resentful spirits here, no restless ghosts. They're not angry anymore. It's okay to forgive yourself."

Something fractures inside Shae. He doesn't know if Arthur's right. He's spent so long hating himself for this. But he *wants* to believe, and that's closer to forgiveness than he's ever gotten before. Maybe it's fitting that he had to come back and hear that here, in front of the house his parents built. He needed to taste the ashes again.

He needed to tell the story out loud to release it from his heart.

After managing to free one hand from Arthur's stupid hot grip, he rubs his stinging eyes. "I really hate you," he mutters. "Fuck. We don't have time for this, I need to—"

"Yeah." Arthur leans down and steals a kiss. A feather-light blaze against Shae's lips, searing him to the core. "Let's banish that demon."

$$ \mathrm{)O(} $$

SHAE SITS IN front of Arthur in the saddle, fingers tangled in a death grip in Duchess's mane as the mare lopes forward beneath him. Her long strides eat up the countryside, and Shae would have fallen off immediately if Arthur's strong arms weren't around him, his broad chest pressed tight to Shae's back. Even the overwhelming, musky scent of him can't ease the twisting in Shae's stomach.

They don't head for the tower. Worry drives them south and east towards Lanwatch. It's the largest collection of souls within fifty miles, and after his long imprisonment, Izen will be hungry.

Shae wants to trust the Charaini border defenses, but he's been self-absorbed for too long. He can't let anyone else get hurt by his recklessness.

Arthur agrees immediately, because of course he does. He's far too good for Shae.

"Are you doing okay?" Shae asks. He's worried about Arthur's stitched-up arm.

Arthur laughs, the sound rumbling through Shae's entire body. "I should be asking you—*Radiance.*" His laughter disappears. Now, all Shae feels is tension at his back. "I feel something up ahead."

He reins Duchess in so sharply that Shae jerks forward in the saddle. They're at the very edge of the dark forest. Dizzy, he looks up and sees a plume of shadows in the sky above, just as one of his rings flares. The shadow twines like a serpent in the sky, winding back and forth in the same place. Occasionally it pushes forward, and blue magic sparks around it.

The Charaini wards are still holding strong.

"I guess we don't have to warn Lanwatch," Shae says, his mouth dry. "If he gets in…" More people will die.

"The city's not defenseless, and the order is close enough to realize something's happening. They can provide backup, and demons are their specialty," Arthur says. "What happens if they kill Izen before you can banish him?"

Shae's breath hitches. All right, maybe he should have been a bit *more* self-centered. That hadn't even occurred to him, in the rush of everything happening. "If he dies on this plane of existence, I'm stuck with these powers forever. I'm stuck with the cold." He twists around in the saddle, trying to look up at Arthur. "We need to go, maybe we can get there before he breaks in. I need to get close enough to cast the banishing."

But Arthur doesn't kick Duchess forward. "He seemed interested in you, when we ran into him on the road," Arthur says slowly. One of his hands drops to Shae's thigh, burning through his clothing. "Can you draw him away from the city instead?"

Shae takes a shaky breath. His throat hurts. He remembers cold, rotten lips on his, nausea surging through him. His voice is tight when he answers, "I think so."

It's time to stop hiding.

They dismount in a clear spot of dirt and low grasses. Incongruously bright wildflowers pepper the land with yellow and white. Shae lands shakily and wants to lean on Arthur forever for support, but forces himself to pull away. He clears a hard patch of earth with his foot and starts rolling up his sleeve with practiced movements.

Arthur grabs his wrist before he can draw his knife.

The harsh words ready on Shae's lips melt away at the intensity in Arthur's eyes.

"I really don't like watching you do that," Arthur says. "Can you use my blood instead?"

The stitches are still visible past his torn sleeve, white thread against red, raw skin. Shae can't tell whether he wants to laugh or cry. "I've spilled enough of your blood today."

"This?" Arthur flexes his arm. "That's barely anything. Here." He scratches one of the smaller cuts on his arm, breaking open the scab.

Shae's stomach flips, torn between nausea and overwhelming affection. Is this how sick Arthur felt watching him cut himself? Somehow it's different when it's Arthur's skin, not his own. "Fine," Shae whispers, then holds out his hand and switches to Lyrisenian. "Life's blood, come to me."

He nearly loses his nerve when Arthur grunts in pain. But he holds steady, unwilling to waste this gift. Blood spills from Arthur's arm and pools into a coin-sized sphere, floating in midair. It reflects and holds the cloud-filtered sunlight. Like it's the brightest color in the landscape.

Shae fumbles a vial from his belt pouch. The blood floats into it. "If I need more, I'm taking my own."

"Sure." Arthur shouldn't be smiling right now, but he is. "What should I do now?"

Shae takes a deep breath. Shadows and blue light still flash back and forth above, testing each other's strength. "Can you put up one of your paladin wards? I'll draw his attention and then start drawing the banishing array. I just need you to hold him away until it's ready."

Arthur leans in and kisses him, soft and quick. "I can do that," he says, and starts walking a wide circle around them. Duchess stands very still nearby, her ears pricked southwards, entirely uninterested in grazing. Magic glitters in the air around and above them as Arthur walks, until they're encircled in a barely visible dome of shimmering gold. It's stronger than the wards Arthur's used before.

Shae waits until he feels the warmth of Arthur's magic wash through him, then starts taking off his rings.

It's more difficult than he expected. Mentally, at least. He's worn some of these rings for nearly ten years, adding more every time he realized there was something new to hide from, something new to detect ahead. He's taken them off to renew the spells, or to change rings when his hands grew, or when he could afford better silver, but it's been at least nine years since his hands were completely bare.

He drops the first ring to the ground. The one that detects ghosts. Then the one that detects demons. The rings fall to the ground with barely a sound, and Shae's hands stay steady, the same steadiness he relies on when closing dead eyes and laying bodies to rest.

The last three all have the same purpose. Silver bands set with ruby and onyx and jade, all enchanted to hide his soul from scrying. Shae tears them from his fingers and flings them aside. Remnants of magic shiver over his skin.

"Izen," he says, with calm he doesn't feel. The name feels far more dangerous without his rings to hide him. "We need to talk."

The air crackles around them, invisible energy snapping through the clearing. The sky above and the flowers below seem to dim. Shae looks south. The distant spiraling shadow stops, then turns towards them.

"Arthur?" Shae says, no longer calm. He's still mad at Arthur. Or at least, he wants to be mad. But he isn't. Arthur came back to him, when he didn't have to. For a selfish moment, he regrets drawing Izen away from Lanwatch. He'd rather save Arthur instead of anyone else.

Arthur glances over his shoulder. "Yeah?"

Neither of them has a chance to say anything else before red-black light flashes around them, and a figure appears at the edge of the ward. Then another.

And another.

Three. Five. A dozen shambling corpses, all with dull, dead eyes and bloody weapons in their hands. Swords, axes, shovels. Men and women who should have slept in the earth, dragged up and twisted into a demon's puppets.

Shae falls to his knees. He pours the vial of Arthur's blood into his palm and begins drawing the array.

ARTHUR

The corpses can't enter the ward. No, it's more than just a ward spell. It's a full shield protecting them, and Arthur's never cast such a powerful spell before. He feels giddy with the power coursing through him, even as he keeps a close eye on the corpses. They throw themselves against the shield over and over, their gray, rotting limbs slapping against the divine magic. Smoke hisses from them where the dark magic animating them reacts to the holy power.

They're loud. Constant growls and moans and single words, coughed-out syllables. A flash of blue catches Arthur's attention, and his stomach twists. On the other side of the barrier waits the mercenary captain, Georgia Oakven. Sword in hand, she stands behind the other corpses as if supervising their movements. She looks nearly alive, except for her death-pale skin and the gaping hole in her chest. Like something punched through her heart and left nothing there.

"Radiance," Arthur breathes.

Georgia prowls in a circle, moving more gracefully than the other corpses. Every once in a while, she touches the barrier, then retracts her hand. Her slow, studied movements are far more frightening than the other corpses' frantic flailing. She's the real threat now.

Arthur adjusts his grip on his sword and circles with her.

She lunges forward suddenly, sword out and streaming with dark energy. The shield rings like a bell when she hits. It holds, but Arthur *feels* the impact in his bones, and he knows this is a waiting game. One of them will tire first, and it's unlikely to be the undead mercenary.

That's fine. He just needs to hold out until Shae's done chanting behind him.

The sun darkens above them, and Arthur looks up to see the great shadow-cloaked serpent coiling above. As it plunges towards them, Arthur prays that Shae can finish this quickly.

The shield reverberates with the impact, but holds. The shadow lands in a plume of dust, crushing several of the corpses beneath it. Smoke and shadow billows away, leaving a tall, dark-cloaked figure.

He very clearly isn't human. He's far too tall, at least a foot taller than Arthur, and his skin is pewter gray. Horns curl back from his temple into sharp onyx points.

Behind Arthur, there's a sudden thunder of hooves. Duchess flees in the opposite direction, breaking past the corpses and heading for the tree line. Arthur's heart sinks in ice. Nothing's ever scared her that badly—but he's also desperately glad she's gone.

The demon's blood-red gaze cuts right past Arthur, fixated on Shae kneeling at the center of the shield.

"How kind of you, Shaesarenna." His lips hardly seem to move, yet his raspy voice echoes all around them. "You've brought such a bright soul for me to eat."

Behind Arthur, Shae's words briefly falter.

"You can go ahead and try," Arthur says, stepping more directly between them.

Izen smiles. His teeth are sharp. "He's not even half-way done with the spell," he tells Arthur. "You won't survive to the end of it."

He lifts his hand, and Georgia flings herself at the barrier again. Other corpses fling themselves against it too. The shield flares with light and power, and Arthur knows he can't maintain such a large spell structure for long, even with the new strength he's gained since leaving the order.

There's an easy solution to that. Arthur takes a deep breath, adjusts his grip on his sword, and makes the shield smaller. It shrinks until it spans just ten feet around Shae.

Leaving Arthur outside of it. He hears Shae's spell-casting falter again, in the brief instant before the hum of the barrier drowns it out.

Three armed corpses lunge toward him, rotting teeth bared. Arthur mutters a prayer, and light flashes around him. The radiance forces them back, their dead skin smoking. Arthur can barely spare any attention for them. He brings up his sword and pivots to meet

Georgia's. Her hair is matted with dirt and blood, and her eyes are pitch black, without sclera.

She presses in viciously, and it's all Arthur can do to keep her from the barrier while still watching Izen. Her undead strength is greater than it should be, but there's a clumsiness to her movements that Arthur doubts she had in life. That clumsiness gives Arthur the edge he needs to save his own skin.

All the while, Izen is still just standing there.

"You like to make others do your dirty work, don't you?" Arthur shouts out to Izen. "Can't take me yourself?"

Cold laughter echoes around the landscape. "Quiet, paladin. I'm speaking to my necromancer."

Fear shivers through Arthur's veins. He doesn't know whether Izen's bullshitting or whether he's actually telepathically harassing Shae, but nothing the demon's doing can be anything good. Arthur parries another blow of Georgia's. "He's not yours, and he won't listen to you."

Izen gives an exaggerated sigh. There's a shimmer of dark magic in the air, and a shadowy sword appears in his hand. Tendrils of black and red smoke waft from its blade. "Alas, you're right. I was bargaining for your life, but it appears he's unwilling to compromise."

Suddenly, Georgia disengages, backing away with her death-pale face turned towards the demon.

The wind picks up, stinging Arthur with specks of dirt and blood and magic. *Radiance*, he prays, and light flares around him, but it's not enough. He can't hold the barrier and protect himself at the same time.

As Izen looms forward, shadow blade raised high, Arthur chooses to hold the barrier.

SHAE

Izen's words creep into Shae's mind. It's nearly impossible to continue chanting the banishing spell with the demon's threats and promises dancing through his heart.

Take your place by my side. Be obedient, and I'll let your pretty paladin live.

Shae doesn't trust the promises, but he trusts the threats. He keeps chanting, with his hands in the center of the circle drawn in Arthur's blood. Power courses through him. Not necromancy, but simple witchcraft, the sort he was born with, the sort he used to summon Izen in the first place. The earth is wet and real against his palms, but he doesn't feel grounded. He's unmoored and scared.

Izen must be scared too, if he's trying to bargain. Shae just has to finish the spell, and everything will be fine.

So stubborn, Izen sighs in his mind. *That's all right. I like you that way.* There's a whistling, rushing sound. Shae glances up and sees the wind swirling around the shield barrier. Arthur's figure staggers through the golden light and the windswept dirt, and a dark blade suddenly appears in Izen's hand. Fear spikes through Shae's heart as Izen drawls, *And his soul will taste so, so sweet.*

The demon lunges forward in a blur of shadow. Light flares, and Arthur's sword flies from his hand. Arthur's on his knees, then on his back, and Izen's sword is coming down, and Shae still has three lines of the spell left to recite. There isn't enough time.

Shae doesn't even think before breaking off the spell. He screams a single word, both a spell and a prayer: Arthur's name.

It rips from his throat with all the force and magic he possesses. He flings out his hand, and power pours into his grasp. Different magics all combining—the coldness inside him. The dark obedience in the nearest corpses. The blood in the earth. The radiance of Arthur's god. The barrier dissolves around Shae, spiraling through the darkness he holds, strengthening and sharpening it.

He flings the spear of power towards Izen's heart and feels the impact in his own chest. The moment hangs. The sword vanishes from Izen's hand, and he arches in a rictus of pain. A scream pours from his throat and roars hell-bound through the air, as great an impact as Shae's bolt of power. Izen freezes into the scream, cracks of red and black appearing in his gray skin.

His sword vanishes. The rest of him turns to ash and crumbles away.

Ears ringing, Shae scrambles to his knees, then his feet. Falls back to his knees. Finds his feet again and staggers forward, past fallen, twitching corpses, to where Arthur lies.

Shae collapses at his side, so dizzy he can barely see anything besides the blood. He reaches for a pulse—and Arthur grabs his hands.

The grip is tight and warm, and relief blooms through Shae's chest. He takes a rough, painful breath. "Are you all right? You're hurt, I thought you were—"

"I'm fine," Arthur says roughly, his voice clearing Shae's head. His eyes are open.

"You don't look fine, you're covered in blood." Shae pulls his hands from Arthur's grasp and starts touching him, feeling his living warmth, cataloguing every cut and scrape he can find. There aren't as many or as bad as he feared, but he's still in a heightened state of anxiety. He's afraid to believe that Arthur's okay. "Let me look at you."

"I said I'm fine," Arthur says, almost laughing, and sits up, heedless of Shae's fluttering. He grabs Shae, both hands on his face to hold him still. The heat of his touch pierces through Shae's heart. "We're both fine," Arthur says, and kisses him.

Only when Arthur's lips cover his, sharing breath and warmth and love, does Shae believe him.

He's reluctant to pull away, and whines a little when Arthur breaks the kiss and starts touching his shoulders, his arms, his sides. Silently checking Shae over for injuries too, Shae's pretty sure, but he doesn't call Arthur out on his hypocrisy. He's too thrilled and grateful that

Arthur's still here, still with him, to touch him like this. He never wants this to stop.

"Did it work?" Arthur asks, and Shae's eyes widen.

He broke off the spell and killed Izen without banishing him. All the power Izen granted Shae remains on this plane, still hooked into his soul. He'll carry this darkness with him the rest of his life.

He should be devastated, but he isn't.

"It doesn't matter," he says, laughing because it's true. All this work, all this pain and desperate effort, for a failed spell, and he doesn't care. "No, it didn't work. I couldn't banish him in time, so I killed him."

Arthur exhales sharply and pulls Shae into a tight embrace. "Radiance, Shae. I'm sorry. I couldn't hold him off long enough."

Shae melts into him, coasting on the high of Arthur's proximity, the relentless drum of his heartbeat. "It's my fault," he says fiercely. "I waited too long to deal with this, and the array broke. This was a stupid plan. But I'm serious. It doesn't matter."

"We'll find another way," Arthur says. "There are mage healers in Ostaris, or we could even try to find an Enoran temple in Praia. There has to be another way to help you."

A wave of affection washes through Shae. He laughs and grabs Arthur's beautiful face to force him to look at him. "*I don't care.* I can live with this power," Shae says quietly. "I've done it for ten years. And I think I've been lying to myself that I'd be okay, and everyone would stop hating me, if I just got rid of it. Nothing's that simple, right?" He leans in for a brief breath of a kiss, then whispers, "I can live with this power, but I don't want to live without you."

Arthur's breath hitches. He touches Shae's face, his lips, with trembling, callused fingers. "What a coincidence," he says, a smile slowly spreading across his face. "I'd say the same to you." He kisses the corner of Shae's lips. Then his forehead. Every touch is sweeter than sunlight. Then he pulls back and starts digging around in his belt pouch.

A moment later, Shae is glad he's already sitting down, because when Arthur looks at him again, he's holding a ring.

It's beautiful. Gleaming silver and yellow topaz. Almost as bright as the look in Arthur's eyes.

"When the hell did you buy that?" Shae says, his voice gone high with shock.

Arthur laughs, low and rich, and Shae wants to sink into the sound forever. "I bought it in Hannick," he answers, smiling. "It reminded me of you. I thought you could embed a spell in it or something, and I meant to give it to you just as a normal gift."

"Do you normally give rings to people?" Shae asks. "Wait, in *Hannick*? That was weeks ago! You barely knew me!"

"I knew you enough that I wanted to make you happy," Arthur says. "And yeah, I realized pretty quickly that this wasn't a normal gift. So that's not why I'm giving it to you now." He swallows, and his smile drops to a more serious expression. "Shae."

Panicking, Shae covers Arthur's mouth with both hands. "Before you ask anything of the sort," he says sternly, "we both need baths, and you need to see a healer. I can't think about anything in this condition."

Arthur laughs under his hands. Kisses his palm. "Fair enough. Will you take the ring now anyway?"

Shae feels himself flushing. "Yes," he says, the warmth tickling through his veins. "Yes, okay."

He lets Arthur take his left hand, currently bare, and slide the silver band onto his fourth finger. The metal is already warm from Arthur's touch. It fits perfectly.

The wind whistles around them, carrying the scent of ash and blood and dead flesh. The sky is bright blue above the scattered corpses, and Shae is the happiest he's ever been.

Then a familiar female voice creaks from behind them. "Moon Mother's tits, what the fuck is going on here?"

ARTHUR

Arthur leaps to his feet in a surge of adrenaline, placing his body between Shae and the voice. He's utterly drained and his sword is ten feet away, but that doesn't matter. There's no way he's letting anything hurt Shae now.

He thought all the walking corpses had lost their power after Izen fell, but one of them is now getting to her feet. The Riverswords blue streak in her hair is unmistakable—which is bad. Arthur could barely fight off Georgia with his sword, much less without it.

But Georgia doesn't move any closer after standing. She puts both hands on her hips and looks around. "Fuck," she says contemplatively. "That was a trip and half."

Her face is still death-pale, and there's still a gaping wound in the center of her chest. But her eyes aren't the same pitch-black as when they fought, and she's making no move to threaten them.

"Don't move," Arthur says, perhaps redundantly, and walks slowly sideways to pick up his sword. He feels better with it in his hand, and better still that Shae follows him, a light hand on the back of his arm.

"I'm not going to bite," Georgia replies. "I don't know what that demon bastard did to me, but I didn't want to fight you then and I don't want to fight you now."

Arthur's too exhausted to try a truth spell, and he's not sure it works on dead people anyway. "What do you think, Shae? This is more your area of expertise than mine."

Shae steps out from behind him, touching his chin in thought. The new ring on his finger gleams in the sunlight. "Can I touch your wrist?" he asks Georgia. "I want to see something."

"I like a man with manners," she says easily. "Though not as much as this guy likes you, clearly. You really know how to pick a moment, paladin."

Arthur's not so sure about that. He feels more like the moment picked him.

He follows at Shae's side as he steps towards the dead mercenary. Georgia herself stays perfectly still, which is smart because Arthur is ready to chop her hand off if she makes the wrong move towards Shae. He can't help tensing as Shae takes her wrist and murmurs something Arthur doesn't understand.

Maybe Shae would be willing to teach him a few words of Lyrisenian.

"The compulsion ended when Izen died," Shae says, still holding Georgia's wrist. "But the animation should have ended too… I think he used a full revival on you. I don't know why."

Georgia asks, "There's a difference?"

"It's complicated," Shae says.

Arthur gestures to the other collapsed corpses surrounding them. "It's the difference between whatever they are and whatever you are."

"Okay, maybe not so complicated." Shae lets go of her wrist and twists his own hands together. He only has the one ring to fiddle with right now. "Captain Oakven, I'm so sorry I got you into this mess. This is— awful. I know. I can lay you to rest when you're ready."

Arthur aches at the way Shae's voice trembles. He reaches down and grabs his hand, and Shae squeezes it fiercely back.

But Georgia just laughs. "Let's take a rain check on that, darling. Do either of you have a shirt I can borrow? Maybe a comb?"

"What?" Arthur asks in disbelief.

She plucks at her blood-stained shirt, torn open around the hole in her chest. "I need to cover this up before I ride back into town. People will talk."

Arthur puts his hand on his sword hilt. "I don't think bringing you back to town is a great idea."

"Wait," Shae says, putting a hand on Arthur's. There's still a tremor in his voice. He turns to Georgia. "You don't want to rest?"

"Fuck no," she says easily. "I've got a crew to take care of, and they already call me heartless. If I turn crazy again, Reed will chop my head off, no problem."

There's a strange expression on Shae's face, but he nods. "Okay. It's your choice." Then he turns to Arthur, his eyes squinting up like he's about to cry. But he smiles instead. "Let's get out of here."

Arthur would like nothing more.

))O((

THEY CLEAN UP the battle site as best they can before leaving. Shae gathers up as many of his rings as he can find and insists on burning the corpses, while Arthur prays over them. Georgia steals a mostly intact shirt from one of them and changes into it. With the gaping hole in her chest covered, she looks ill but not dead.

Duchess returns midway through their work, snorting unhappily at the smoke. Arthur buries his face in her neck, inhales, and starts to feel like himself again instead of a dazed, impulsive fool.

He keeps looking at the new ring on Shae's finger, though, and doesn't regret being impulsive at all.

"I thought you two broke up," Georgia says, as Arthur kisses Shae's temple for the dozenth time. "This is insufferable."

"I'd say I'm sorry," Arthur says with a grin, "but I'm really not."

He's still overwhelmed by the fact that Shae gave up his goal for him. He cursed himself to a lifetime with this harsh power. Arthur vows silently to do everything he can to make that easier.

They set off for Lanwatch, Arthur and Shae riding double and Georgia walking beside them. She doesn't seem to tire at all. Shae spends most of the ride asking her questions about various sensations and perceptions, and Georgia sometimes answers. It's slow going, and nearly dark when they meet the group of guards and crown's mages outside the border gate.

The mages are casting into the barrier, testing it or strengthening it or something. The guards swarm forward to confront the three travelers.

"How do I look?" Georgia asks, brushing her hair back.

"Mostly alive," Arthur answers.

Then Arthur is selfishly grateful they didn't lay her to rest, because she strides forward and handles all the talking. The way she tells it, the three of them valiantly saved the city from a rogue demon and attacking corpses. They were in no way responsible for causing the problems, Georgia was not one of the attacking corpses in question, and the Riverswords will be charging an exorbitant amount of hazard pay to the Lanwatch council. Of course Shae and Arthur are in her employ, she's known them for years.

Arthur's not thrilled with the lies, but he's too tired to come up with anything better.

A guard runs off midway through her explanation, and by the time they finally ride into the city, a small crowd is gathered. Arthur's not surprised to see more soldiers and mages, a few Riverswords, and he picks out the councilmembers by their fine clothes and the brass torques around their necks. He *is* surprised to see a number of familiar sun-emblazoned tunics—Captain Tanner, Freya, and a few other sisters and brothers.

Former sisters and brothers.

Shae stiffens at the sight. "Do you need to talk to them?" he asks quietly.

"I probably should," Arthur says. "But we can avoid them if you want."

Shae sighs. "No, I think I've learned my lesson about avoiding things."

Arthur hugs him tight, then dismounts and helps him down. A nearby guard takes Duchess from Arthur, and then there's nothing between them and Captain Tanner. Arthur steels his nerves and takes Shae's hand as they walk over.

"Captain," he says. "I thought you were heading back to Ostaris."

"Most of them are on their way, but Karis scried out some trouble here so I brought a few people back around." Tanner sighs. "I should have known something was really going on when you left, Arthur. You've always had good instincts."

"With a few exceptions?" he can't help asking.

Behind her, Freya laughs. Tanner's lip just twitches a little. "Good battle instincts," she says gruffly. She looks away briefly, as if the next thing she has to say is something very difficult. "Look. I might have been a bit hasty with you the last time we spoke. I think that given what happened today, we could make a good case for your reinstatement. I'd hate to lose one of my best men over all of this."

Arthur stares. It's the closest thing to an apology he's ever heard her give. And for a moment, he's tempted to accept. To ride back to the Bright Cathedral, his brothers and sisters at his side, to renew his oath and serve the Radiant Order.

Only for a moment. Because nothing's truly changed since he left, except that Arthur knows he made the right choice. Tanner's being nice to Arthur now, but she hasn't even looked at Shae once.

Arthur doesn't need an organization that's more concerned with looking good than doing good. He doesn't need an organization that wants to force him to choose between faith and love, when he knows his god wants him to have both. His contract with Vara doesn't depend on the order after all, and it's stronger than ever now that he's making his own choices.

"I appreciate that, sir," he says, squeezing Shae's hand. "But I meant it when I quit. Vara has another path for me."

Tanner frowns, then sighs again. "Suit yourself, Arthur. And good luck."

Shae's hand clenches suddenly. "Wait a second," he says, wide eyed. "You left the order?"

Arthur laughs. "I guess I was too busy to mention that, but yeah." He takes Shae's other hand too and spins him around so they're facing each other, and the heat that cascades between them is warmer than anything Arthur's ever felt. In front of everyone—paladins, soldiers, mercenaries, Vara only knows who else—he bends down to murmur in Shae's ear, "I'm all yours now."

"What are you doing?" Shae hisses. "You shameless—"

But when Arthur kisses him in the middle of the street, he kisses back just as eagerly.

Shae

It's another couple of hours before they end up their accommodations for the night, a spare room in the Riverswords outpost. Arthur's injuries have been tended by a mage healer—the deepest ones can't be fully healed, but they're healed enough not to need stitches—and Shae relented to aid for his own injuries too. Most of his bruises were just from continually falling off his horse. He's happiest to have the fingerprints around his neck eased away, cleansing Izen's touch from his skin.

They take separate baths down the hall, because Shae rather liked kissing Arthur in public, but he's not quite prepared to give their hosts a complete show. And he needs the moment of solitude, washing off the blood and grime, to start feeling like himself again, without the distraction of Arthur's touch.

He still doesn't feel quite clean or safe until he's alone with Arthur. The room is simple, with whitewashed walls and unstained wooden furniture. There's a table, chairs, and washbasin at one end of the room, and a wide, red-quilted bed at the other.

There's Arthur Davorin, standing in the doorway with his boots still on, looking at Shae like he's the most amazing thing in the world.

Shae doesn't feel amazing. He feels raw and shattered, and he has no idea what the rest of his life is going to look like. But he wants to live up to the adoration in Arthur's eyes.

"Well, we've bathed and healed, and I think it's time we really talked." Shae sits on the edge of the bed and starts to unlace his boots. "We reached Lyrisenia, and I dealt with the demon. Not quite how I planned, but you fulfilled the terms of our contract."

Arthur closes the door behind him. Locks it with an audible click. "Are you firing me, necromancer?"

The word doesn't sting when Arthur says it so fondly.

"Maybe." Shae kicks away his boots and tilts his head up as Arthur draws nearer. The man's so tall. "I was thinking, since we worked so well together, that I wouldn't be opposed to a new contract."

Arthur laughs and kneels next to the bed, between his thighs. The scent and heat of him fills every inch of Shae's awareness. He takes Shae's left hand and runs his thumb over his knuckles. Lingers on the topaz and silver ring. He says, voice low and resonating through Shae's very bones, "Marry me, Shae."

Shae knew what he was going to say already, but hearing the words is still a shock. He feels warm all over, and his throat chokes up. He wants to say something important, something eloquent about how much he wants this and how much he loves this brilliant man, but the only word he can manage is, "Yes."

Arthur's grin is brighter than the sun. Shae only has an instant to be dazzled by it before the man surges upwards and kisses him. They fall back against the bed, Arthur's body firm over his, grounding him purely in this moment. Shae gasps into Arthur's lips, opens up to a deeper kiss, and forgets that he was ever cold.

They break apart enough to shed their clothes, clumsy with desperation. The moment Arthur takes to find the denseed oil feels like an eternity, but in the next breath, Arthur's kissing him again, running a warm hand down his chest. His thumb circles around Shae's nipple, drawing out a whine Shae wouldn't have believed came from his own throat if he didn't feel it with a primal need.

"Come here." Arthur sits up against the pillows and draws Shae into his lap. Shae ruts against him, their cocks sliding together in sparks of pleasure. Arthur groans, and his hand tightens on Shae's hip. He's so beautiful like this, all powerful muscle and strength and that chiseled jaw, unraveling in desire for *Shae*.

"Let me," Shae says, taking the jar from Arthur. He dips his fingers in the oil and strokes it over Arthur's length. His own cock jumps in arousal at the feel of Arthur's in his hand, hot and slick and heavy, and at the way Arthur's breath grows more ragged with every movement. Any nervousness Shae had about not knowing what he was doing burns away in the heat of Arthur's gaze.

He spends less time prepping himself—his own fingers are far less interesting than the slick, hard cock in front of him. A few cursory pumps are all he manages before rising up on his knees and then sinking down.

"Fuck, Shae, take your time," Arthur gasps, grabbing him by the hips to support him.

"Do I have to?" Shae teases.

His confidence is his downfall, though, and he drops down too quickly. He whimpers, seeing stars, with the impact of Arthur's cock at this angle, filling him so completely. There's an edge of pain. He doesn't dislike it, but he's too overwhelmed to move or breathe or do anything.

Arthur leans up to kiss him, and all the tension unravels. When Shae can move again, he rocks up and down in tiny increments, unwilling to pull too far away. He wants to be this close forever. So close he can't tell which of them is moving more, which of their heartbeats is louder in his ears. Whether there's any difference in the breath shared between them.

When they finally collapse together, utterly spent, Shae can only curl up against Arthur's chest and savor the scent of him. Somehow, Arthur has enough energy to stroke through his sweat-stained hair, a soothing, gentle touch.

Shae's eyes squeeze shut. He says, "Thank you for coming back."

Arthur's hand pauses in Shae's hair. Then resumes. "I always will."

Shae falls asleep to Arthur's touch, and knows that it's true.

EPILOGUE
ONE MONTH LATER

"Have you thought about my offer?" Georgia asks. She's sitting on a chair in the kitchen of the little house Shae and Arthur just moved into. The house is outside of Lanwatch, close enough that Shae can run over if he's low on living energy, but far enough out to keep Duchess and Sparrow in a nice open field out back. Arthur says he's going to hire help to build a small shelter before winter hits. In front, there's a garden that Shae has absolutely no idea what to do with.

Shae sets aside his focusing crystal and lets go of Georgia's wrist. He sits down in the chair across from her. "Yes, I talked about it with Arthur, and we don't want to join the Riverswords completely, with a guild contract and all. But we're happy to work with your crew on relevant jobs."

"Great." Georgia stretches out her arms. She's dressed in ordinary leathers, and her eyes are as bright as ever. The pallor of her skin is the only sign that under her leather jerkin, there's a hole where her heart should be.

Another voice sounds from the doorway—Reed, her second in command, with his arms crossed as usual. "Has she gone crazy yet, necromancer?"

"Not yet," Shae says, tucking his focusing crystal back into his belt pouch. "Her energy's stable, and I think it'll stay that way unless something drastically changes."

"That's good," Reed says gruffly.

Georgia laughs, standing up. "Are you worried about me, darling? You're going soft. I won't have that."

"Don't think I won't cut your head off if I have to, sir," he gripes back. But Shae's gotten to know them enough over the past few weeks that he hears the affection in both of their voices.

He wasn't expecting Georgia's troop to accept her new undead status quite so easily. He also wasn't expecting Georgia to still be standing and sane after a month. They've been meeting multiple times a week for Shae to examine her and make sure she's not a ticking time bomb of undead malice. So far, so good.

He's found a strange comfort in it, though he hasn't managed to voice it to anyone yet, even Arthur. The fact that raising the dead might not always be a disaster, that some dead people might want to stay awake for a little longer. Ten years ago, his parents chose to rest again, but they could have chosen to stay. Shae wouldn't do it over again, of course, but he doesn't feel quite as guilty anymore for giving them that choice.

"Where's your man, by the way?" Georgia asks.

Shae's face heats, and he hopes his flush isn't too obvious. By the snort from Reed, his hopes are in vain. "He's in town saying good-bye to the other paladins."

Most of the troop had left soon after the aborted demon attack, but Freya and Harry had stayed for the past month. Whether their aim was to help the Lanwatch guard or get in their way depended on who Shae spoke to.

Georgia wrinkles her nose. It's clear where her opinion lies. "Good riddance."

Shae doesn't think all the paladins are that bad, anymore, but he's still not excited to talk to them. He declined when Arthur asked if he wanted to go into town with him today. Two months ago, he might have gone, prickling and nervous that Arthur might change his mind again and decide to ride off with the order.

Now, he doesn't need to. He trusts Arthur to come back to him, always.

🌛🌕🌜

ARTHUR RETURNS NOT long after Georgia and Reed leave. The afternoon is still bright, and Shae is barely starting to feel the usual chill of being alone. Ever since the events a month ago, the cold hasn't come on as quickly as it used to. He still hasn't figured out whether that's due to the array breaking or Izen dying—his connection to one or both of them must have been more of a drain on his soul than he thought.

While Shae doesn't enjoy the occasional shiver, he's used to it. He's certainly suffered worse. And it makes the wave of warmth as Arthur's aura washes over him all the sweeter.

Shae hears hooves outside and doesn't look up from the packets of seeds on the kitchen table. They're unlabeled, and he's trying to remember which is supposed to be carrots and which are flowers. This garden is going to be such a disaster.

It always takes Arthur a while to untack and groom Duchess, and he usually ends up giving Sparrow an extra curry too while he's out there, and feeding them far too many treats. Shae had asked one of the stablehands when they picked Sparrow back up, and the stablehand confirmed that Arthur gives his horses an unusual number of cookies. So Shae sets the seeds aside and goes to sit on the back step, watching his lover play with the horses.

They haven't decided when or where to marry yet. Shae still wants to find a ring for Arthur, and Arthur isn't sure what church to use. He wants to find time to visit his family too. They have all the time in the world to figure that out, though.

"How'd everything go?" Shae asks, when Arthur finally closes the gate and walks up to the house.

Arthur's smile brightens when he meets Shae's gaze. "Everything's good. They're heading back to Ostaris." He reaches down and lifts Shae to his feet. "How about you? Did you miss me?"

Shae leans in against him. "Yes," he says, winding his arms around Arthur's neck. "I missed you terribly."

Arthur kisses the corner of his lip, drawing back with another smile. "How can I ever make it up to you?"

"I have a few ideas." Shae drags him in for another kiss, this one deeper, slower. He's breathless when he pulls away, his whole body tingling with the taste. "You'll have to tell me if I ever get too clingy, you know."

"I like you clingy." Arthur grabs both Shae's hands, enveloping them in warmth. Lifts the left one up, so the ring catches the bright afternoon sunlight. It's dazzling. "Have you decided what spell to put in this one yet? You promised not to bleed on it."

"I promised not to bleed on it *on purpose*," Shae corrects quickly, then laughs at Arthur's brief glare. He squeezes Arthur's hands and brushes a kiss to his cheek. "I decided not to enchant it. It's perfect already."

Arthur laughs too. "When did you become such a romantic?"

"You're one to talk," Shae accuses. Because sure enough, Arthur's the one who sweeps him off his feet and carries him inside.

Shae still wears other rings for concealment and detection. He has most of his old earrings in too, for control and protection. Even without Izen lurking to the north, he's always going to need them, because he's always going to be a necromancer.

But that doesn't mean he has to be alone. Not anymore.

MIDWINTER LIGHTS

A RADIANCE SHORT STORY

The days shorten faster in Lanwatch than in Port Charain or Ostaris. Arthur still isn't quite used to the exaggerated seasons. Summer is nice; he likes the extra daylight. But a couple years after settling into their new home, Arthur is still adjusting to the northern winters.

One thing is the same in Port Charain, Ostaris, and Lanwatch, though. The Midwinter Festival is the highlight of the winter.

The festival isn't dedicated to any one god. Certain Varan priests say it's an opportunity to beseech and praise Radiant Vara, to pray for sunlight's return and longer days. Sephinian priests say it honors Mother Sephine, though they argue about whether or not fertility rituals should be part of that honoring. Maizans claim the festival is a celebration that the previous autumn's harvest is enough to get communities through the winter—and certainly, lean autumns result in far more modest solstice celebrations.

Arthur thinks Songbird's bard-priests have the greatest claim to the solstice. Without their songs and stories, winters would be far darker all across Charain.

A week before this year's festival, when they're in town to get some shopping done, a chalked wooden sign catches Arthur's attention. He pauses outside the bakery. "I think I want to enter that."

Shae stops with him. The wicker basket on his arm looks incongruous with his dark coat, and the silver rings bright against his fingerless gloves. He's never tried to hide that he's a necromancer, even though he probably could, now that he has Arthur. "Really?"

"Really," Arthur says. "It'll be fun."

Shae frowns. Looks between Arthur and the sign a few times. "Have you ever made a pie before? Even once?"

"No. Have you?"

"No," Shae says immediately. "But that doesn't matter, because I'm not the one who wants to enter a Midwinter Festival pie contest."

Arthur sighs. "Where is your sense of adventure?"

"In a tomb somewhere, probably." Shae's tone is frosty, but Arthur can see the amusement dancing in his gray eyes. Shae turns, his boots crunching in the thin layer of snow. "Don't expect me to help you on this fool's mission, but I'm willing to taste-test your experiments."

"Have I told you today how amazing you are?" Arthur asks with a laugh. "How handsome, gracious, and understanding?"

Shae glances over his shoulder, a barely-there smile on his lips. "You may have mentioned it a few times. But feel free to keep going."

"Tolerant, handsome, clever, hilarious, handsome—"

☽○☾

SMOKE BILLOWS FROM the oven. Shae slumps over the table, laughing his ass off, while Arthur rushes from window to window. Cold winter air rushes in, and dark, burned-sugar smoke wafts out.

"I don't understand," Shae says through tears of laughter. "You can cook other things perfectly fine. Your roast chicken last week was incredible. Why have you murdered seven pies in a row?"

"Murdered is a strong word." Arthur opens the kitchen door for good measure. Out in the backyard, Duchess and Sparrow have their ears pricked towards the chaos in the cottage.

"Would you prefer mutilated? Destroyed? Desecrated?" Wiping his eyes, Shae makes his way towards the oven to peer at the charred, smoking pie in the brick oven. "I think this pie is beyond even my powers of resurrection."

Arthur wipes his hands on his green cotton apron. Pure happiness colors his chagrin. Sure, this has been a terrible waste of flour and apples. And his chances of even getting a pie to the Lanwatch Midwinter Pie Contest look slimmer by the day. But Shae's laughter is addictive.

He never could have imagined that the dour, prickly necromancer he met in Andell would turn out to be so full of joy.

"All right, I have enough flour left for three more crusts."

"No," Shae says sternly. At least, he's clearly attempting to be stern, as his lips keep twitching into a grin. He comes up behind Arthur and starts untying his apron. "No more pies. You are *forbidden* from entering the pie contest. We'll be run out of town."

"Do you think so?" Arthur reaches back and grabs Shae's wrists. Pulls them around his waist, into a hug, more or less.

"Absolutely." Shae leans his cheek against Arthur's back. His arms tighten around Arthur's waist. "They've tolerated my necromancy for well over a year now. I refuse to further darken my reputation by becoming an accessory to baking crimes."

"You're paranoid," Arthur says.

"You're in denial," Shae counters. But he can't say anything else because Arthur turns around. Pushes him back against the wall, and kisses him senseless.

As the smoke clears, Arthur's the happiest man in the world.

☽○☾

THEY ARRIVE IN Lanwatch in the early evening, as the sun lingers over the horizon. Small lanterns are strung between the regular street lamps, making a canopy of light over the fresh-swept town streets. More lanterns sit in the windows of every open shop and most of the houses. The lights illuminate the faint flakes of snow drifting through the air.

Most of the activity is in the town square, but booths and tables of food and activities spill out into side streets too. Lanwatch seems more alive, less empty than usual, with everyone out in the streets.

Arthur and Shae stop by the stables first, to board Duchess and Sparrow for the evening, then make their way towards the Riverswords outpost. Laughter, cheers, and shouts of dismay ring out from inside. Arthur takes Shae by the hand, feeling the warmth of his fingers and the chill of his rings, and enters the outpost.

About half of the Lanwatch Riverswords gather by the fire. The usual couches and armchairs are cleared away in a circle, leaving the focus on a small table and two chairs. In one chair sits Captain Georgia Oakven, head thrown back in laughter. In the other slumps Darren, a cheerful young mercenary Arthur's worked with before over the past year. Darren covers his face in his hands, then accepts a flask from the middle-aged woman behind him.

"Drink your defeat, boy," Bricks says.

"You have to drink double, my dear!" Georgia shouts. "That's what you get for challenging me twice."

"I know, I know!" Darren steps back from the table with a laugh, shaking out his arm. "I'll be back in an hour—next time for sure! Fuck, first I lose the pie contest, now this…"

Arthur spots Reed, Georgia's second in command, mixing a punch bowl of something at the lobby's front desk. With Shae at his heel, he heads over to say hello. "What are they doing over there?"

Reed pours them each a mug of steaming liquid. Mulled wine, by the smell. "Right, you weren't here last year. This is our annual midwinter arm wrestling contest." He shakes his head. "It was a bit more of an actual contest before Georgia, well, died that one time."

Shae sips his wine, looking over as Bricks challenges Georgia next. "Yes, the undead strength would make that an unfair contest. I'm surprised anyone takes her up on it."

By this point, each of Georgia's darlings knows their captain is undead. Hiding it from the townsfolk is one thing, but her Riverswords live close together, and they're fervently loyal. Arthur's never met another troop of Riverswords with quite the same rapport. It sometimes reminds him of what he used to feel in the Radiant Order, before he left.

Reed shrugs. "It's tradition. And she's got all of them wrapped around her cold, clammy finger."

"All of *them*?" Arthur asks with a grin. Of all the mercenaries in Georgia's troop, Reed's quiet, constant loyalty runs the deepest.

Reed shakes his head and reaches under the desk for another bottle to pour into the punch bowl. The alcoholic fumes are enough to sting Arthur's eyes— and the brew in his hand is already plenty strong. Best to stick to one cup for now.

"I think I'll give it a go," Arthur says, after setting aside his empty mug.

He half expects Shae to caution otherwise, but Shae just smiles slightly. "Radiance guide you."

Five minutes later, Arthur's arm slams into the table. Georgia counts to three, then releases her grip and whoops in triumph. "That's a dozen for the night! Does anyone else dare challenge their captain?"

"Radiance, I wouldn't," Arthur says with a grin, even though he just did. Shaking out his arm, he stands up to accept his forfeit from Bricks. "Happy Midwinter, Captain."

"And a happy fucking Midwinter to you too," Georgia says cheerfully. "A woman's got to find her pleasure somehow, when she can't drink anymore. Come on, who's up next?"

A slight figure steps out from Arthur's shadow and takes the chair. "I think I need to defend my husband's honor," Shae says.

Wolf whistles ring out throughout the room. Georgia laughs. "That's adorable. You're on."

Concern twists through Arthur's gut—Shae's skinny arms are hardly in shape for arm wrestling ordinary mercenaries, much less undead ones. But Shae grins up at him, and Arthur can only grin back.

Shae put up with him murdering a total of eleven pies over the past week. Arthur owes Shae support for his own bad ideas too. "You've got this, love."

With a slight grin, Shae rolls up his right sleeve, and places his elbow on the table. Georgia clasps his hand with a grin of her own.

Bricks counts off as the referee. On three, the pair of clasped hands starts trembling—and Shae mutters a few words in Lyrisenian.

Wisps of shadows wind their way around Georgia's arm. She swears, but can't react before Shae pushes her arm to the table with a *thunk*.

There's a moment of silence, before every mercenary in the room starts laughing. "You cheated!" Georgia accuses, but she's laughing too. "Necromancy is cheating."

"Wait, this is supposed to be a *fair* contest?" Shae says. "If I'm cheating, so are you."

"You got me there." Georgia sighs, and looks longingly at the flask in Bricks's hands.

Warmth spreads through Arthur's spirit, sweeter and stronger than the mulled wine. He likes the place they've found up here, and the way Shae fits in with everyone. He likes seeing Shae make friends. Amidst all the laughter, Arthur claps Georgia gingerly on the shoulder. "I'll drink the forfeit for you."

"Nightven should drink it," Georgia says, her dead eyes sparkling. "As his penalty for cheating."

After brief negotiation, Arthur and Shae share the flask.

) O (

THEY VENTURE BACK into the town square, buying a bag of candied walnuts to share. Arthur looks regretfully at the bakery, where the pie contest entries can be seen through the golden-lit windows.

"Next year will be your year." Shae hooks one arm around Arthur's. He's been in a good mood since the arm wrestling contest. Even the side-eye from the farmer selling the candied nuts didn't put a damper on his mood.

Gaining the rest of Lanwatch's acceptance has been slower than the Riverswords. Nobody's rude, and plenty of people are friendly, but some suspicions linger. Over the past year and a half, Arthur's started to pay more attention to the way people look at Shae—while Shae seems to care less and less with every passing month.

"Darren said they do a different baking contest every year," Arthur says. "Maybe next year, I can murder cakes instead."

Off to one side of the town square, a bard-priest perches on a barrel. Her fingers are nimble on the strings of her lute, despite the cold weather, and instead of singing, she trades riddles with her audience as she plays. The gathered listeners are mostly children, with parents chatting off to the side.

Arthur and Shae stop at the back of the crowd to listen while they finish the walnuts. A few children look back briefly, before refocusing on the bard-priest's music. One girl with long red braids under her knit blue hat looks the longest, wide eyes focused on Shae.

A few songs later, the bard-priest hops down from the barrel and sweeps a bow. "Thank you, thank you, and a happy midwinter to everyone! Who's next, for song or story?" She points to a few of the adults in turn. "You, sir? Fair lady? Perhaps you?"

The small, red-haired girl jumps up and points to the back of the crowd. "The necromancer should tell us a ghost story!"

Everyone freezes. "I'm not sure that's a good idea," one man says, with an awkward laugh. He scratches his head under his wool hat, the same blue as the little girl's hat. "Sorry, my daughter's a bit obsessed with ghosts right now."

"Ghosts are *awesome*," the tiny girl says enthusiastically.

The surprise on Shae's face is almost funny. Arthur's about to open his mouth and make a polite excuse to leave—he doesn't want Shae put on the spot—but then an older girl, around eleven or twelve years old, chimes in.

"Anyone who's *scared* can go play games with the other babies." She glances at the other twelve-year-olds next to her, who look very impressed. "I want to hear Mister Necromancer's story."

"We don't want to bother him," another parent says.

To Arthur's surprise, Shae laughs and waves his hand, so his silver rings gleam. "It's no trouble. I can tell a story if you promise you won't be too scared."

"We won't!" the children chorus. The little girl who spoke up first yells the loudest.

"Are you sure?" Arthur whispers quietly. He wants to be a supportive husband, but arm wrestling a friendly walking corpse is one thing. Giving the neighborhood children nightmares is quite another.

"Trust me," Shae whispers back. He squeezes Arthur's hand, then moves to the front of the audience and hops up on the barrel. "My name is Shae," he says, smiling slightly. "Though Mister Necromancer is fine too. Now, the story begins on a winter night like tonight, seven years ago..."

Five minutes later, Arthur and the nervous parents realize they needn't have worried. Shae's tale is full of spooky ghosts—but even more full of academic theory and the principles of spellcrafting. When he starts describing the reason he used the silver spoon instead of the silver knife that he found in the haunted house, Arthur sees several of the children nodding off.

The children are disappointed; the parents are thrilled. The man in the blue hat sidles up to Arthur, and says quietly, "Tell your husband thanks. I thought I'd never get my daughter to fall asleep tonight."

"Of course," Arthur says, unable to quell his grin. Maybe Shae's already closer to fitting in here in Lanwatch than Arthur thought.

He takes the opportunity as Shae is occupied to slip away, just for five minutes.

)O(

AFTER THEY GET home and take care of the horses, they find a box waiting on their back step. Tendrils of warm air rise visibly from the corners, wafting into the wintery night and illuminated by the mote of sunlight Arthur has hovering above their heads.

"Stay back," Shae says, grabbing Arthur's arm. "I don't sense anything demonic, but you never know."

"It's not demonic." Arthur laughs and tugs Shae forward. "I asked Darren to deliver it."

"Can't be too careful. He's not very sensible—oh, that smells *good*."

The warm scent of apples and cinnamon hits their noses as they reach the step. All caution gone, Shae kneels down and lifts the lid of the paper box. Arthur moves the mote of sunlight over, revealing a gloriously gleaming buttery crust, perfectly crimped edges—even shaped dough flowers decorating the top. A paper heating charm is folded in the corner of the box, keeping it piping hot despite sitting on the porch for hours. The only imperfection in the pie is the one missing slice.

"I wanted to compensate you for, well, everything I did to our oven this week, so I bought this from Darren," Arthur says. "He won second place in the contest. The missing slice is from the judges."

"Is that where you went while I was story-telling?" Shae straightens up, pie in hand, and tilts his face up.

Arthur takes the invitation and kisses him—only briefly, before Shae pulls away.

"I'm putting this safely on the table before we do anything else," he says sternly. "I need *one* pie in this kitchen to survive the Midwinter Festival."

Arthur puts his hands up in surrender, and waits until the pie is safely away before sweeping Shae into a deeper kiss.

ABOUT THE AUTHOR

Tavia Lark writes m/m fantasy romance and erotica. Her favorite romance tropes include hurt/comfort, sharing a bed, and enemies to lovers. She writes from a sunny little apartment with the constant "help" of her fluffy cat. He just really likes typing, okay.

KEEP IN TOUCH

Website: www.tavialark.com
Newsletter: www.tavialark.com/list
Patreon: www.patreon.com/tavialark
Group: www.facebook.com/groups/tavialark